Private Pages

THE DESCENT OF ERIKA LAWRENCE

JULIE FREEBUSH

SFD PUBLICATIONS

Contents

CHAPTER ONE

Invisible

*D*ear diary,

    Another birthday spent staring at the clock. Another year older, another night alone.

The candles on my cake melted into sad little puddles while I waited. Michael texted at 7:30—"Sorry babe, big client meeting running late. Start without me?"

Start without him. The story of our marriage these days.

I poured myself a second glass of the expensive cabernet I'd bought for us to share. The bottle made a hollow sound when I set it back down. Like our dining room. Like our house. Like the promises.

"It's just temporary," he said last month. "Just until the Anderson merger." Before that it was the Peterson account. Before that,

something else. The names change but the empty chair across from me remains the same.

I blew out my own candles at 8:45. Thirty-five years old. Made a wish I'm embarrassed to admit even to these pages.

Mom called around nine, asked if we were "celebrating in style." I lied. Said Michael had taken me to that new bistro downtown. That he'd surprised me with earrings. That we were drinking champagne. Why burden her with the truth?

The cake was actually good. Devil's food with buttercream frosting from that bakery on Elm. I ate two slices while watching reruns of Friends. The one where Rachel turns thirty. At least she had people around her.

His keys jingled in the door at 11:37. I pretended to be asleep on the couch. Felt his kiss on my forehead, smelled the scotch on his breath. Heard him whisper "Happy birthday" before he headed upstairs.

I should have said something. Should have asked why his client meeting smelled like Macallan 18. Should have asked if he remembered what day it was before he walked through the door.

Instead, I stayed still. Counted the ticks of the grandfather clock in the hall. Wondered when exactly we became two people sharing an address instead of a life.

Tomorrow I'll smile when he gives me whatever last-minute gift he picked up. I'll say I love it. I'll pretend today wasn't today.

But right now, at midnight on my birthday, I'm allowing myself this moment of truth:

I'm tired of starting without him.

I woke up to the sound of Zach's alarm blaring through the wall—that ridiculous heavy metal song he insists helps him "transition into consciousness." Three snooze cycles later, I was already in the kitchen scrambling eggs and checking Lily's math homework while she frantically searched for her volleyball knee pads.

"Mom, have you seen my—"

"Laundry room, blue basket, already washed them." I slid her plate across the counter without looking up from the polynomial equations. "You switched a negative sign on number seven."

Lily groaned, mouth full of toast. "I hate polynomials."

"You hate everything before 10 AM," Zach mumbled, shuffling into the kitchen with his hair defying gravity and eyes barely open. His growth spurt hit last month—suddenly my baby boy towers over me, all elbows and Adam's apple, his voice cracking between octaves.

"Science project due today?" I asked, already knowing the answer.

His eyes widened. "That's Friday, right?"

"Thursday. Today is Thursday."

The look of panic was worth the price of admission. I reached behind the refrigerator and pulled out his carefully wrapped solar system model we'd finished at midnight two days ago.

"Take it out to the car. You're welcome."

His relief transformed into a rare, genuine smile—the kind that's becoming endangered as teenage coolness takes over. "You're the best, Mom."

"Tell me that when I make you clean your room this weekend." I handed him his lunch bag. "Peanut butter, no crust, extra strawberry jam. And yes, I included those disgusting sour candy things you like."

Michael wandered in as I was herding the kids toward the door, already dressed for work, already on his phone. He kissed my cheek absently.

"Parent-teacher conferences tonight," I reminded him. "Six o'clock."

"Right, right," he nodded, not looking up from his screen.

Lily rolled her eyes dramatically behind his back. I shot her a warning look, though secretly I appreciated her solidarity.

We performed our daily exit choreography—backpacks, water bottles, permission slips signed, phones checked for battery life. I straightened Zach's collar and wiped a smudge of toothpaste from Lily's chin.

"Love you, monsters," I called as they tumbled out the door.

"Love you too," they replied in teenage unison—Lily's sincere, Zach's reluctant but present.

Some days they're the only ones who see me at all.

I watched Michael pour his coffee into his travel mug, his movements mechanical, practiced from years of the same morning routine. He hadn't looked directly at me once.

"I might be late tonight," he said, scrolling through emails on his phone.

"Parent-teacher conferences, Michael. We talked about this last week." I kept my voice even, though something hot and tight coiled in my chest. "Mrs. Hernandez specifically asked to meet with both of us about Zach's English grade."

He glanced up, brow furrowed. "Can't you handle it? The Anderson account is—"

"The Anderson account." I nodded, cutting him off. "Right. The same account that made you miss Lily's volleyball championship. And Zach's science fair. And my birthday dinner."

His eyes finally met mine, surprised by the edge in my voice. I rarely pushed back.

"Erika, you know how important—"

"I know exactly how important everything is." I turned away, loading dishes into the dishwasher with more force than necessary. "I'll tell Mrs. Hernandez you're unavoidably detained. Again."

Michael set his phone down, and for a moment I thought he might actually engage. Instead, he checked his watch.

"We'll talk about this tonight, okay? I need to go."

I didn't turn around as he approached. His lips brushed the back of my head—not even my cheek, just my hair—before he grabbed his briefcase.

"Don't wait up," he called, already halfway out the door.

The house fell silent. I stood motionless in the kitchen, surrounded by the evidence of a family I'd fed and clothed and organized, feeling strangely hollow. The morning sun streamed through the windows, illuminating the granite countertops I'd insisted on during the renovation three years ago. Everything looked perfect, magazine-worthy.

I caught my reflection in the microwave door—faded and distorted. When had I become this woman? This ghost who moved through rooms making beds and signing permission slips, invisible except when something went wrong?

I picked up Michael's abandoned coffee mug from the counter. He'd left it there despite the dishwasher being open right beside it. Fifteen years of marriage, and he still couldn't see what was right in front of him.

CHAPTER TWO

The Mirror

Erika stood in front of the full-length mirror mounted on her bathroom door, her body bare in the harsh overhead light. The children were at school, Michael at work, and the house wrapped around her in empty silence. This solitude granted her the rare luxury of truly seeing herself.

She turned sideways, eyes tracing the subtle curve of her stomach. Not flat anymore—not like before the kids—but still relatively firm. Her hand brushed across it, feeling the slight softness that remained despite hundreds of crunches and planks she would perform three times weekly.

"Thirty-five," she whispered to her reflection.

Her breasts had changed too. Once high and proud, they now yielded slightly to gravity's persistent pull. Still attractive, she thought, but different. Changed. Like everything else.

Erika's gaze traveled down to her thighs, where faint silvery lines marked the rapid expansion of her body during pregnancy. Battle scars, her friend Natalie called them. Proof of life created. Erika had once embraced that sentiment. Now she wasn't so sure.

She turned, examining her backside over her shoulder. Not bad. The squats were paying off at least. Her eyes caught a glimpse of gray at her temple—when had that appeared? She leaned closer, fingers separating strands of hair to better see the betrayal of time.

"You're being ridiculous," she told her reflection, but continued her inspection.

Her face showed the beginnings of lines around her eyes and mouth. Laugh lines, they were called, though Erika couldn't remember the last time she'd laughed hard enough to warrant them deepening. The slight hollowing beneath her cheekbones wasn't entirely unwelcome—it gave her face definition—but it was another reminder of passing years.

Erika stepped back, taking in the complete picture. This body had carried two children. It had been desired once, touched with reverence and hunger. When was the last time Michael had looked at her—really looked at her—with that heat in his eyes?

She placed her palm flat against the cool surface of the mirror, as if reaching for the woman on the other side. The woman who was her, but somehow separate too. A stranger wearing her skin, watching her life unfold from the outside.

Erika pulled on her robe, tying it loosely at the waist as memories washed over her. How different things had been in those early days.

Ten years ago, they'd barely made it through the front door of their first apartment. Michael had pressed her against the wall in the narrow hallway, his mouth hot against her neck, hands already working at the buttons of her blouse.

"We should unpack," she'd laughed, not meaning it.

"Later," he'd murmured against her skin. "Much later."

They'd christened every room of that tiny one-bedroom walk-up before a single box was unpacked. The kitchen counter. The bathroom sink. The living room floor because they couldn't wait to assemble the bed frame.

Erika smiled at the memory as she wandered into their bedroom—their current bedroom, spacious and tastefully decorated, with a king-sized bed that now seemed too large, too empty. She ran her fingers over Michael's pillow, remembering how he used to wake her on Sunday mornings, his hands sliding beneath her nightshirt, his lips tracing patterns down her spine.

"You're so beautiful," he'd whisper, voice rough with sleep and desire. "I can't believe you're mine."

Once, during their third year of marriage, before the kids, they'd been grocery shopping—such a mundane task—when Michael had suddenly abandoned their cart, grabbed her hand, and pulled her out to the car.

"What are you doing?" she'd asked, laughing as he practically shoved her into the passenger seat.

"I can't wait until we get home," he'd said, his eyes dark with hunger. They'd driven to a secluded spot overlooking the city and made love in the backseat like teenagers.

Erika sank onto the edge of the bed, the memory so vivid she could almost feel his hands on her again, the urgency of his touch, the way he'd looked at her as if she were the most desirable woman in the world.

When had that changed? When had the passionate man who couldn't keep his hands off her transformed into someone who barely seemed to notice when she walked through a room?

Erika's phone buzzed on the nightstand, startling her from her reverie. Natalie's name flashed on the screen. She hesitated before answering, still half-lost in memories.

"Hey, stranger," Natalie's voice came through, bright and energetic as always. "How was the big birthday? Did Michael surprise you with something amazing?"

Erika shifted on the bed, tightening the belt of her robe. "Oh, you know. He had to work late."

The silence on the other end spoke volumes.

"Again?" Natalie finally asked, her tone carefully neutral.

"It's fine. He's got that big project..." Erika trailed off, suddenly tired of making excuses for him. For them. "Actually, no. It's not fine."

"I knew it." Natalie's voice softened. "Listen, I'm taking you out tonight. No arguments."

Erika glanced at the family calendar hanging on the wall. Nothing was scheduled except Zach's soccer practice, then the parent teacher conference.

"I don't know, Nat. The kids—"

"Are teenagers who can survive one evening without you hovering. When was the last time you did something just for yourself?"

Erika couldn't remember. That was the problem.

"Fine," she conceded. "But nothing crazy. I'm not twenty-two anymore."

"Thank god for that. Your twenties fashion choices were questionable at best," Natalie laughed. "I'll pick you up at seven thirty. Wear something that makes you feel sexy."

After hanging up, Erika stood and walked to her closet. She pushed aside the practical blouses and slacks she wore for bookkeeping clients, the comfortable mom-jeans and sweaters that comprised her daily uniform. In the back, partially hidden behind winter coats, hung outfits from another life. A life before carpools and PTA meetings and keeping track of everyone's schedule but her own.

Her fingers brushed against a black dress she hadn't worn in years. Simple but elegant, with a neckline that hinted rather than revealed. Michael had loved this dress. Once.

Erika pulled it from the hanger and held it against herself, turning toward the mirror again. Maybe it was time to remember who she had been before she became everybody's everything. Before she became invisible.

Chapter Three

Girls' Night

The bar hummed with life—a stark contrast to the quiet house Erika had left behind. Neon lights cast a pink-blue glow across the sleek surfaces, transforming ordinary faces into mysterious strangers.

"Another round?" Natalie slid an empty martini glass away and signaled the bartender with practiced ease.

Erika hesitated, fingers still wrapped around her first drink. "I should probably pace myself."

"It's your birthday celebration." Natalie leaned closer, her perfume cutting through the bar's mingled scents. "When's the last time you did something just for you?"

The question hung between them as the bartender placed fresh cocktails on the polished counter. Erika couldn't remember.

"Michael has that conference call with Tokyo tonight, and Zach has that history project due—"

"Stop." Natalie placed her hand over Erika's. "Just for tonight, they don't exist."

"That's a terrible thing to say."

"Is it? You've spent fifteen years being someone's wife, someone's mother. Tonight, you're just Erika."

The music shifted to something with a deeper bass that Erika felt in her chest. Two men at the end of the bar glanced their way. The taller one smiled at her.

"Don't look now, but we've caught some attention." Natalie took a deliberate sip of her drink.

"They're probably looking at you."

"Trust me, that guy in the blue shirt hasn't taken his eyes off you since we walked in."

Heat crept up Erika's neck. "I'm married."

"I'm not suggesting you take him home. Just... remember what it feels like to be seen."

Erika took a larger swallow of her drink than intended, wincing as it burned down her throat. "I wouldn't even know how to flirt anymore."

"It's like riding a bike." Natalie tossed her hair back. "Besides, half the fun is just knowing you still could if you wanted to."

"Michael used to look at me like that." The words slipped out before Erika could catch them.

Natalie's expression softened. "When's the last time you two went out? Just the two of you?"

Erika stared into her glass. "Valentine's Day. Last year."

"That's what I thought." Natalie clinked their glasses together. "So loosen up. Dance with me. Laugh too loud. Stay out past your bedtime."

"The kids—"

"Are teenagers who can microwave their own dinner for once."

Erika took another sip, smaller this time, letting the warmth spread through her chest. The music wasn't so bad. The bar wasn't so intimidating. And for the first time in longer than she could remember, she felt a flutter of something like possibility.

Erika excused herself to the restroom, weaving through the crowded bar. At the sink, she caught her reflection—cheeks flushed, eyes brighter than they'd been in months. She washed her hands, the cool water a brief respite from the bar's heat.

As she dried her hands, her wedding ring slipped off, landing with a soft clink in the sink. Erika froze. The platinum band had grown loose over the years—another small change she'd never bothered to fix. She picked it up, turning it over in her palm, the weight familiar yet suddenly conspicuous.

On impulse, she tucked it into her purse's inner pocket instead of sliding it back on.

"Just for tonight," she whispered to her reflection, echoing Natalie's words.

The bar seemed different as she made her way back—or perhaps she moved differently through it. A man shifted to let her pass, his eyes lingering on her face, then dropping briefly to her bare left hand. He smiled, the gesture unhurried and deliberate.

"Can I buy you a drink?" he asked, his voice just loud enough to carry over the music.

"I'm with a friend," Erika replied, surprised at how steady her voice sounded.

"Both of you then." His eyes never left hers.

"Maybe next time." She moved past him, heart racing with an unfamiliar thrill.

Back at their spot, Natalie was chatting with the bartender. Erika slid onto her stool, suddenly aware of the empty space on her finger—a small absence that felt enormous.

"You okay?" Natalie asked, pausing mid-sentence.

"Fine." Erika reached for her drink. "Just... experimenting."

Natalie's eyes dropped to Erika's hand, her eyebrows rising. "Bold move."

"It fell off in the bathroom." Erika took a sip. "I thought... I don't know what I thought."

"I noticed you caught someone's attention on your way back."

"He asked to buy us drinks."

"And?"

"And nothing. I said no."

Natalie nodded. "But it felt good to be asked?"

Erika's silence was answer enough. Across the bar, another man caught her eye, his gaze dropping to her hand before meeting her eyes again with newfound interest.

"I forgot what this feels like," Erika admitted quietly.

The night shifted into something dreamlike when the bartender placed a fresh cocktail in front of Erika—one she hadn't ordered.

"From the gentleman at the end of the bar," he explained, nodding toward a man in a charcoal suit.

"I can't accept—" Erika began automatically.

"Sure you can." Natalie nudged her. "It's just a drink, not a marriage proposal."

The man approached before Erika could decide. Up close, he was older than she'd initially thought—mid-forties, with salt-and-pepper hair and laugh lines around his eyes.

"I hope I'm not intruding." His voice carried a slight accent she couldn't place. "I'm Daniel."

"Erika. And this is Natalie."

He acknowledged Natalie with a polite nod but kept his attention fixed on Erika. "I noticed you weren't wearing a ring anymore when you came back from the restroom."

Heat flashed across Erika's face. "You're observant."

"Professional habit. I'm a photographer." His eyes swept over her face with deliberate appreciation. "You have remarkable bone structure."

Natalie coughed into her drink, poorly disguising a laugh.

"That's... thank you." Erika took a sip from the drink he'd sent, the unfamiliar cocktail sweet with an unexpected kick.

"Let me guess," Daniel leaned against the bar, close enough that she caught the scent of his cologne. "Recently divorced?"

"No, I'm—" She stopped herself. Tonight, she was just Erika. "Just taking a night off."

His smile deepened. "Interesting answer."

"Is it?"

"Very." He moved closer, his knee brushing against hers. "Most women would simply say they're married."

"Most men wouldn't notice a missing ring."

"I notice everything about beautiful women."

The compliment landed with surprising weight. When was the last time someone had called her beautiful and meant it? Michael used to whisper it against her skin, but those moments had faded into quick pecks and distracted "you look nice" comments.

"What else do you notice?" The question slipped out, bolder than she intended.

"That you're not used to this anymore." His eyes held hers. "Being seen. Being wanted."

The directness of his gaze made her pulse quicken. She was acutely aware of Natalie watching their exchange, of the press of strangers around them, of the wedding ring tucked away in her purse like a secret.

"And what if I am married?" Erika asked, surprising herself.

Daniel's smile never wavered. "Then he's a very lucky man who should remember that other men notice what he has."

"I appreciate the drink and the compliments," Erika said, sliding the glass away slightly. "And maybe if I wasn't married..."

She paused, feeling the weight of the words. "But I am, and I do need to get back home to the kids."

Daniel's smile turned knowing, his eyes still holding that appreciative gleam. "I respect that. But who knows, maybe I'll see you here again some night."

"You never know," Erika replied, surprised by the hint of possibility in her own voice.

She slipped off the barstool, steadier than she expected after the cocktails. Natalie followed suit, exchanging a quick glance with Erika as they gathered their purses.

The cool night air hit Erika's flushed face as they pushed through the exit doors. The street was quieter than the bar's interior, though still alive with passing cars and distant laughter.

Natalie burst into laughter once they were safely on the sidewalk. "You did good in there! See? You've still got it."

Erika fished in her purse, fingers finding her wedding ring. She slipped it back on, the familiar weight settling against her skin. "It did feel good," she admitted, flexing her fingers as if reacquainting herself with the band. "To be noticed like that. To be wanted."

"That's all I wanted you to remember." Natalie linked her arm through Erika's as they walked toward the parking lot. "That you're more than just someone's wife and mother. You're still you."

The streetlights cast long shadows ahead of them. Erika's heels clicked against the pavement, the rhythm somehow more confident than when they'd arrived hours earlier.

CHAPTER FOUR

Waking Up

Erika's house greeted her with the same silence she'd left behind. She kicked off her heels at the door, the click of the lock echoing through the empty foyer. Michael's text—"Working late, don't wait up"—had arrived during her ride home.

The clock on the microwave read 11:47. She moved through the kitchen, turning on lights as she went, illuminating spaces that somehow felt different now. Had the distance between the kitchen island and the refrigerator always been so vast? Had the family photos on the wall always shown smiles that seemed so practiced?

She poured a glass of water and leaned against the counter. The house was clean—she'd spent the morning scrubbing it—but now she noticed dust on the baseboards, a smudge on the stainless steel refrigerator door. Imperfections she'd overlooked before now screamed for attention.

Upstairs, she checked on the kids. Zach sprawled across his bed, one foot hanging off the edge, headphones still clamped over his ears. She gently removed them, tucking the blanket around him. In the next room, Lily slept curled on her side, her chemistry textbook open beside her.

The master bedroom waited at the end of the hall. Erika paused at the threshold, suddenly seeing it with new eyes. Michael's side of the bed was pristine, untouched for days. Her nightstand overflowed with half-read books and moisturizer. His held only a charging cable and a glass of water from three days ago.

When had they stopped sharing the small details of their days? When had "I love you" become just words mumbled into phones between meetings?

She changed into her pajamas and slid under the covers, the emptiness of the king-sized bed suddenly oppressive. Daniel's words echoed in her mind: "Being seen. Being wanted."

She reached for her phone, scrolling through messages. Nothing from Michael beyond his terse work update. She pulled up their text history—practical exchanges about groceries, the kids' schedules, bill payments. When was the last time he'd sent something just because he was thinking of her?

The house creaked and settled around her. Erika stared at the ceiling, hyperaware of the hollow space beside her, of the silence where conversation should be, of the distance that had grown so gradually she hadn't noticed until someone else had reminded her what it felt like to be truly seen.

Erika lay in bed, the moonlight casting long shadows across the room. The sheets were a tangled mess around her legs, a testament to her restlessness. She glanced at the clock—it was late, or early, depending on how you looked at it.

The faint sound of the front door closing sent a ripple of anticipation through her. Michael was home. She listened to the familiar cadence of his footsteps on the stairs, the soft murmur of him checking on the kids. It was a dance they'd done a thousand times, but tonight, it felt like a performance for an audience that had long since left the theater.

He entered their room, his tie loose, the top button of his shirt undone. He looked at her, his eyes heavy with fatigue or maybe something else—something Erika couldn't quite place.

"You're still up," he said, his voice low, almost a whisper.

"I waited for you," Erika replied, her own voice steady despite the flutter in her chest.

Michael nodded, a silent acknowledgment, before he turned to the walk-in closet to change. Erika watched him, the lines of his back etched with the weariness of the day. She remembered a time when those lines were drawn by laughter, by passion, by the sheer joy of being in each other's company.

He emerged in his pajamas, his eyes avoiding hers as he made his way to his side of the bed. Erika's heart thrummed in her chest, a steady, yearning drumbeat. She rolled onto her side, reaching out to touch his arm.

"Michael," she began, her hand tracing the curve of his bicep, "I missed you."

He stiffened slightly at her touch, a reflex that stung more than any rejection ever could. Erika withdrew her hand, the space between them growing even as they lay side by side.

"It's been a long day, Er—," Michael started, the tiredness in his voice palpable.

"I know," she cut him off, her tone soft but resolute, "but when was the last time we really talked? Or... anything else?"

Michael's gaze finally met hers, and for a moment, Erika saw something flicker in his eyes—regret, perhaps, or the echo of a connection that was slowly slipping away. But then it was gone, replaced by the familiar, gentle mask of a man who was used to putting others first, even at the expense of his own needs.

"I'm sorry, Erika. I just... I can't tonight," he said, the words hanging heavy in the air.

Erika nodded, the motion almost mechanical. She turned away from him, pulling the covers tight around her as she stared into the darkness. The silent void between them seemed to expand, filling the room until there was barely enough space for breath.

Michael switched off the bedside lamp, plunging the room into a deeper shade of night. Erika listened to the steady rhythm of his breathing as it slowed, signaling his descent into sleep. She lay there for a long time, her mind racing, her heart aching with a loneliness that was becoming all too familiar.

Eventually, the edges of her own exhaustion began to blur the sharpness of her thoughts. But as sleep finally claimed her, she held onto the faint hope that tomorrow might bring a different conversation, a chance to bridge the gap that had grown between them.

Dear diary,

I don't know what's wrong with me. Or us. Or maybe this is just what happens to all marriages after fifteen years? The slow drift into separate lives under the same roof.

Michael barely looked at me last night. I reached for him and felt him flinch. FLINCH. Like my touch was unwelcome. When did I become something to avoid? Someone whose affection is a burden?

I remember watching my parents' marriage dissolve into polite conversation and separate bedrooms. I swore I'd never let that happen to us. Yet here I am, the kids at school, Michael at work, alone again writing in this diary because there's no one to talk to.

Natalie says her divorce was liberating. "Better to be alone than lonely with someone else," she told me. Is that where we're headed? The thought terrifies me.

What happened to the man who couldn't wait to get me alone? Who used to text me during meetings just to say he was thinking about me? Now I'm lucky to get a "working late" message.

Maybe I'm expecting too much. We have careers, teenagers, bills, responsibilities. Passion fades, right? That's what everyone says. But does it have to disappear completely?

I keep searching for the moment we changed. Was it when Zach started middle school? When Michael got his promotion? When I stopped making an effort with my appearance because he never seemed to notice anyway?

Last night at the bar, I felt something I haven't felt in years—visible. Desirable. A stranger bought me a drink and looked at me like I was worth seeing. And God help me, I liked it.

Is that terrible? To want to be wanted? To crave that electric feeling when someone's eyes linger on you?

I love my family. I love Michael. But I'm drowning in invisibility here. Suffocating in the quiet politeness of our marriage.

Do all wives feel this way eventually? Do they all lie awake wondering if this emotional desert is all that's left after the early passion dries up?

I don't know what to do. Fight for us? Accept this is just how marriage evolves? Or admit that maybe we've already become strangers who share nothing but an address and offspring?

CHAPTER FIVE

The Gym Decision

The decision materialized while Erika was staring at her bank statement. Her part-time bookkeeping job had built a modest personal savings—money that wasn't earmarked for household expenses or the kids' college funds. Just hers. She'd been squirreling it away for years, though for what purpose, she'd never been entirely sure.

Until now.

The Edge Fitness Club sat nestled between a high-end boutique and an organic café in the trendy part of town where Erika rarely ventured. Its glass façade gleamed in the morning sun as she pulled into the parking lot, her stomach fluttering with an unexpected nervousness.

"First time?" The receptionist smiled, her teeth impossibly white against her tanned skin.

"That obvious?" Erika laughed, tucking her hair behind her ear.

"Everyone starts somewhere." The woman slid a tablet across the counter. "Fill this out while I grab some information packets for you."

Erika glanced around the lobby. Everything gleamed—the chrome, the glass, the polished concrete floors. Even the people looked polished, with their coordinated athletic wear and purposeful strides. Nothing like the community center where she occasionally used the treadmill.

"Our premium membership includes unlimited classes, personal training sessions, and access to the spa facilities." The receptionist returned, laying out glossy brochures. "It's an investment in yourself."

An investment in yourself. The phrase echoed in Erika's mind as she signed the membership agreement. When was the last time she'd invested in herself? Not in her role as mother or wife or part-time bookkeeper—but in Erika, the woman who existed beneath all those labels?

She handed over her credit card, the one connected to her personal account.

"Welcome to Edge Fitness, Mrs. Lawrence."

"Just Erika," she corrected, surprising herself. "Just Erika is fine."

The woman smiled knowingly. "Erika it is. Your first class is tomorrow at nine—hot yoga with Marcus. He's tough but transformative."

Transformative. Another word that lingered as Erika walked back to her car, membership card tucked safely in her wallet. She caught her reflection in the gym's windows—a woman taking a small step toward something new, something that belonged only to her.

Erika arrived for her first yoga class fifteen minutes early, clutching her new mat like a shield. The studio gradually filled with women in coordinated sets and men with easy confidence. She tucked herself into a back corner, unrolling her mat with methodical care.

"First time?" A woman with a gray-streaked ponytail smiled at her.

"Is it really that obvious?"

"Only because you look terrified." The woman extended her hand. "I'm Diane. Been coming to Marcus's class for two years."

"Erika. Is it... difficult?"

"Challenging, but worth it. Just go at your own pace."

The instructor—Marcus—swept in with the energy of a storm front. Tall and lean with close-cropped hair and skin the color of burnished copper, he commanded attention without demanding it.

"New faces today," he noted, his gaze landing briefly on Erika. "Welcome. Remember, yoga isn't competition—it's conversation between you and your body."

The heat intensified as the class progressed. Erika's muscles trembled with effort, sweat collecting along her hairline and between her shoulder blades. She struggled through the poses, occasionally glancing at others for guidance.

During a particularly challenging warrior sequence, she caught a reflection in the mirrored wall—a man two rows ahead watching her. Their eyes met briefly before he returned his attention to his own form. Young, maybe thirty, with the defined physique of someone who made fitness a priority.

When they moved into downward dog, she noticed another man—older, silver-haired, in expensive-looking athletic wear—glance her way. Not leering, but definitely noticing.

The attention felt strange—foreign yet vaguely familiar, like a language she'd once known but had forgotten through disuse. In the concentrated effort of the poses, she'd forgotten to be self-conscious about her body. Her leggings and tank top clung to her curves, revealing rather than hiding.

During the final resting pose, eyes closed on her mat, Erika became aware of something shifting inside her. The burning in her muscles felt good—productive, alive. For sixty minutes, she hadn't been someone's mother or wife. She'd just been a body in motion, present and accounted for.

After class, as she rolled up her mat, she caught the silver-haired man looking again. He nodded slightly—a gesture of recognition, perhaps respect—before heading toward the water station.

Erika floated through her front door, her muscles pleasantly sore, her skin still flushed from the hot yoga class. The house greeted her with its familiar silence—Zach at soccer practice,

Lily at her friend's house, Michael at work. For once, she welcomed the emptiness. It gave her space to savor this new feeling coursing through her veins.

She dropped her gym bag by the stairs and caught her reflection in the hallway mirror. Her cheeks glowed with healthy color. Her eyes seemed brighter, more alive. Even her posture had changed—shoulders back, chin lifted. The woman looking back at her wasn't the invisible wife who'd stared critically at her body weeks ago. This woman had presence.

In the kitchen, she poured herself a glass of water, gulping it down while scrolling through her phone. A notification from the gym appeared—a welcome message with the week's class schedule. Her finger hovered over Marcus's Thursday morning class before tapping to reserve her spot.

Upstairs, she peeled off her sweaty workout clothes and stepped into the shower. The hot water cascaded over her shoulders, and she closed her eyes, remembering the silver-haired man's appreciative glance, the younger man's lingering look. Not creepy or invasive—just male attention that acknowledged her as a woman, desirable and seen.

How long had it been since she'd felt that? Since she'd felt like more than a domestic fixture, a background character in her own life?

She ran her hands over her body—her breasts, her stomach, her hips—with new appreciation rather than criticism. These parts of her that had carried and nourished children, that had weathered time and gravity, were still worthy of desire. Still capable of turning heads.

After her shower, instead of reaching for her usual worn leggings and oversized t-shirt, Erika pulled on a sundress she'd bought last summer but rarely wore. The fabric skimmed her curves, the neckline just low enough to reveal the gentle slope of her collarbone. She applied a touch of mascara, a swipe of tinted lip balm.

Downstairs again, she put on music—not the usual background noise, but something with rhythm and heat. She swayed her hips as she prepared a simple dinner, feeling the lingering stretch in her muscles, the newfound awareness in her body.

For the first time in months—maybe years—Erika felt fully present in her skin, electric with possibility.

CHAPTER SIX

Testing the Waters

The mall's fluorescent lighting cast everything in a flat, unforgiving glow, but Erika didn't care. She moved through the athletic wear section with purpose, fingertips grazing fabrics she'd previously dismissed as impractical extravagances.

"Can I help you find anything specific?" A saleswoman approached, her own outfit a testament to the store's aesthetic—sleek leggings that emphasized her long legs, a fitted crop top revealing a slice of toned midriff.

"Just browsing," Erika started to say automatically, then stopped herself. "Actually, yes. I need new workout clothes. For hot yoga."

The saleswoman—Tory, according to her name tag—nodded approvingly. "Perfect timing. We just got our summer collection in."

Thirty minutes later, Erika stood in the fitting room surrounded by a colorful array of options. She slipped into a pair of high-waisted leggings in a deep teal that hugged every curve without suffocating them. The matching sports bra offered support while showing off her shoulders and the subtle definition beginning to emerge in her arms.

She turned sideways, examining her silhouette. The outfit revealed more skin than she'd shown in public in years. But instead of the critical internal monologue that usually accompanied mirror moments, she heard something different. Something that sounded suspiciously like approval.

At the register, she added a black pair with mesh panels and a crimson set that made her feel like someone who commanded attention. The total made her wince briefly, but she handed over her credit card without hesitation.

"These will look amazing on you," Tory said, folding each piece with care.

The following morning, Erika stood before her bathroom mirror, makeup bag open beside the sink. She hadn't bothered with more than tinted moisturizer for gym sessions before—what was the point of sweating it all off?

But today she reached for her mascara, carefully coating her lashes. A touch of cream blush on her cheekbones. Tinted lip balm that enhanced her natural color.

Subtle enough to look effortless. Deliberate enough to make a difference.

She slipped into the teal outfit, adjusting the sports bra to sit just right. The woman who looked back at her from the mirror wasn't trying to hide or blend in. This woman wanted to be seen.

Natalie slid a ceramic mug across the table toward Erika. Steam curled upward from the dark roast, carrying the comforting aroma of their weekly ritual at Beans & Books, the quiet café tucked between a vintage clothing store and an independent bookshop.

"Okay, spill it." Natalie leaned forward, elbows on the table. "You've been checking your phone and fidgeting since you sat down. And you're wearing lip gloss to coffee. On a weekday."

Erika's hand flew to her mouth self-consciously. "Is it too much?"

"It's perfect. But different." Natalie's eyes narrowed with the practiced scrutiny of a twenty-year friendship. "This isn't just about the gym, is it?"

Erika stared into her coffee. The words she'd rehearsed in her head on the drive over suddenly seemed pathetic when faced with the prospect of actually saying them aloud.

"Michael hasn't touched me in three months." The confession rushed out, barely above a whisper. "Not really. A peck goodbye, maybe a hand on my shoulder when he passes behind my chair. That's it."

Natalie's expression softened. "Have you talked to him about it?"

"I've tried. He says he's tired. Work is stressful. The economy's uncertain." Erika's laugh came out brittle. "As if the economy has anything to do with whether you want your wife."

She traced the rim of her mug with her fingertip. "The other night, I put on that black slip dress he used to love. The one from our anniversary trip to Napa. He glanced up from his laptop long enough to say 'you look nice' before going back to his spreadsheets."

"Bastard," Natalie muttered.

"That's just it—he's not. He's not cruel or mean. He just doesn't see me anymore." Erika blinked back the heat behind her eyes. "Sometimes I wonder if anyone would notice if I just... disappeared."

"I'd notice." Natalie reached across the table and squeezed her hand. "And so would Zach and Lily."

"I know. I didn't mean it like that." Erika took a steadying breath. "But lately, at the gym, men look at me. Actually look. And it feels..."

"Good," Natalie finished for her. "It feels good to be desired."

Erika nodded, guilt and relief washing over her in equal measure at having the feeling named aloud.

"I won't lie to you," Natalie leaned closer, lowering her voice. "After my divorce, when I finally started putting myself first again, it was... transformative."

Erika glanced around the café, suddenly self-conscious about the turn in conversation. "What do you mean?"

"I mean I didn't jump straight into another relationship." Natalie's lips curved into a knowing smile. "I rediscovered parts of myself I'd forgotten existed."

"You're being cryptic."

"Fine." Natalie took a sip of her coffee. "I've had a few casual encounters. Nothing serious, nothing complicated. Just... human connection."

Erika nearly choked on her coffee. "You mean—"

"Sex, Erika. Yes." Natalie rolled her eyes. "Don't look so scandalized. We're not in high school anymore."

"But how do you even... I mean, where do you meet these people?"

"Sometimes at bars. Once at a work conference. The hotel gym, actually." Natalie shrugged. "You'd be surprised how many people are in similar situations. Not looking to blow up their lives, just seeking something that's been missing."

Erika's chest tightened. The idea simultaneously terrified and intrigued her.

"Don't you feel guilty?"

"I did at first," Natalie admitted. "But then I realized I spent eight years feeling guilty for wanting basic things in my marriage. For needing attention, affection. For having desires." She tapped her fingers against the table. "I was done apologizing for being human."

Erika stared into her mug. "I could never—"

"I'm not saying you should. God knows it's complicated." Natalie's tone softened. "But I will say this: there's something powerful about being reminded that you're more than some-one's wife or someone's mother. That beneath all those roles, you're still a woman with needs that deserve to be met."

The words hung between them, charged with possibilities Erika had never allowed herself to consider.

"Does it help?" she finally asked. "Does it make the loneliness better or worse?"

Natalie considered this. "It reminds me I'm alive, and that definitely counts for something."

CHAPTER SEVEN

First Temptation

"Keep your back straight. That's it."

Damon's voice had become a familiar part of Erika's new routine, low and encouraging as he guided her through each workout. Three weeks into her training sessions, and she'd started looking forward to them more than she cared to admit.

"Now lower into the stretch. Slowly."

His hand rested lightly on her shoulder as she bent forward. Even through her workout top, his touch sent a current across her skin. She'd chosen her outfit carefully today—the new matching set in deep purple that hugged every curve she'd rediscovered.

"You're making great progress." Damon crouched beside her, close enough that she caught the clean scent of his aftershave. "Your form has improved dramatically."

"I have a good teacher." The words came out more breathless than she'd intended.

His eyes met hers, held for a beat longer than necessary. "Let's work on your hamstrings next. Lie back."

Erika complied, stretching out on the mat in the private training room. The gym was quieter today—a Tuesday afternoon when most people were at work. Damon lifted her right leg, one hand supporting her ankle, the other just below her knee.

"Relax into it," he instructed, pressing her leg toward her chest. "Tell me if it's too much."

"It's good," she managed, acutely aware of his hands on her body. Professional touches, she reminded herself. This was his job.

He leaned forward slightly, increasing the stretch. "Breathe through it."

His face was inches from hers now. Erika noticed the flecks of gold in his brown eyes, the precise line of his jaw.

"Better?" he asked, his voice dropping lower.

"Yes." She couldn't look away.

As he lowered her leg and reached for the other, his fingers brushed against her inner thigh. The touch lingered a fraction too long to be accidental.

"Sorry," he murmured, not sounding sorry at all.

"It's fine." Her heart hammered against her ribs.

This time when he pressed her leg forward, his hand slid slightly higher on her thigh. His eyes locked on hers, questioning.

Erika didn't pull away. Instead, she found herself arching slightly into his touch.

"Erika..." Her name was a question on his lips.

His hand moved deliberately now, tracing a path along her leg that had nothing to do with stretching muscles.

"We probably shouldn't," she whispered, even as her body betrayed her words.

"Probably not," he agreed, but his hand continued its journey upward.

The moment hung suspended between them. Erika knew she should move away, sit up, say something professional—but her body refused to obey. Damon's fingers traced slow circles on her inner thigh, each one moving imperceptibly higher.

"This isn't part of the usual routine," she managed, her voice barely audible.

His eyes darkened. "No, it's not."

His palm slid upward, fingers splaying against the thin fabric of her leggings. The pretense of a training session had evaporated completely. His thumb brushed against the seam where her thigh met her hip, and Erika's breath caught.

"Tell me to stop," he whispered.

She should. She knew she should.

Instead, she reached up and curled her fingers around his wrist—not to pull his hand away, but to hold it there, against her. The wedding ring on her finger caught the light, a glinting reminder she chose to ignore.

Damon leaned closer, his free hand bracing beside her head. "I've wanted to touch you like this since your first day here."

His confession sent heat pooling low in her belly. How long had it been since anyone had wanted her this way? Since Michael had looked at her with this kind of hunger?

"This is wrong," she breathed, even as her hips shifted slightly against his touch.

"Then why does it feel so right?" His fingers moved higher, bolder now.

The training room door clicked shut somewhere behind them, footsteps passing in the hallway. The sound broke through the haze of desire, snapping Erika back to reality. This was a public place. She was a married woman. This was her personal trainer.

She sat up abruptly, forcing space between them. "I can't."

Damon didn't push. He sat back on his heels, eyes still dark with want but respectful of her boundary. "I understand."

"I'm married," she said, the words sounding hollow even to her own ears.

"I know." He ran a hand through his hair. "And I crossed a line. That's on me."

Erika fumbled with her car keys, hands still trembling. The drive home passed in a blur of conflicting emotions—guilt and excitement battling for dominance. She parked in her driveway, checked her appearance in the rearview mirror. Did she look different? Could anyone tell?

The house was empty. Zach had soccer practice, Lily was at debate club, and Michael... Michael was wherever Michael always was these days. Not here. Not with her.

She dropped her gym bag in the laundry room and headed straight for the bedroom, not bothering to shower away the lingering scent of Damon's aftershave that clung to her skin. Her diary lay in its hiding place beneath her winter sweaters. She hadn't written in it since that last frustrated entry about Michael's rejection.

Erika's fingers still trembled as she uncapped her pen.

Dear diary,

I almost cheated today. The words look strange written down. Alien. I've never been unfaithful to Michael. Never even considered it before. But today with Damon...

His hands on my body felt electric. Not clinical or professional. Deliberate. Wanting. When was the last time someone touched me like they were discovering treasure? When was the last time Michael looked at me the way Damon did today—like he couldn't wait to devour me?

I stopped it. I should feel proud of that, but instead I'm sitting here wondering what would have happened if I hadn't. If I'd let his fingers continue their path upward. If I'd pulled him down to me instead of pulling away.

I'm still throbbing with want. My skin feels too tight. Too sensitive. I keep replaying the moment—the heat in his eyes, the deliberate pressure of his touch, the way he whispered my name like a prayer.

What's happening to me? Am I really considering this? Risking my marriage, my family, for what? A moment of feeling desired?

But God, it felt so fucking good to be wanted. To be seen. To be something other than Zach and Lily's mom or Michael's invisible wife.

I don't know what I'll do when I see Damon again on Thursday. I don't know if I trust myself anymore.

She closed the diary, buried it back beneath the sweaters, and pressed her hands against her flushed cheeks. The house's silence seemed to echo with accusation. But beneath the guilt, a dangerous current of anticipation hummed through her veins.

Thursday was only two days away.

CHAPTER EIGHT

The Car Encounter

"Not tonight, honey. Big presentation tomorrow." Michael didn't even look up from his laptop as he dismissed her, fingers continuing their steady rhythm against the keyboard.

Erika stood in the doorway of their home office, the silk robe she'd put on after her shower suddenly feeling ridiculous. She'd even spritzed on the perfume he used to love. Had he even noticed?

"It's been weeks, Michael." Her voice came out smaller than she intended.

He glanced up, expression softening momentarily. "I know. Things will calm down soon, I promise." Then his eyes returned to the screen, the blue glow illuminating his face in the dim room. "Maybe this weekend?"

The familiar placeholder promise hung between them. This weekend would become next weekend, then the one after that.

"Sure." She tied her robe tighter and retreated, closing the door behind her.

In their bedroom, Erika stared at her reflection. The clock read 7:30 PM. Too early to sleep, too late to call Natalie. She opened her closet, fingers trailing over her gym clothes. The gym closed at 10. She could get in a good workout, burn off this restless energy crawling beneath her skin.

Twenty minutes later, she pushed through the glass doors of Elite Fitness. The evening crowd had thinned, leaving only the dedicated night owls. No sign of Damon—relief and disappointment warred within her. After their encounter two weeks ago, their sessions had been carefully professional, the tension between them a living thing they both pretended to ignore.

"Closing in two hours," the front desk attendant reminded her.

Erika nodded and headed for the treadmill. She ran until her legs burned, until sweat plastered her shirt to her back, until the only thing in her mind was the rhythm of her feet and the beat of her heart.

She moved to the weight room, surprised to find it empty. The wall clock showed 9:15. Most members had cleared out, heading home to partners who noticed them, who wanted them.

"Thought that was you."

She turned to find Damon in the doorway, gym bag slung over his shoulder. He wasn't in his usual trainer gear—just jeans and a fitted henley. Off-duty.

"Just needed to burn off some energy," she said, setting down the weights.

"Everything okay?" He stepped into the room, keeping a respectful distance.

Erika laughed, the sound hollow. "Not really."

Damon's eyebrows lifted. "Want to talk about it?"

"Not particularly." Erika wiped her face with a towel, suddenly self-conscious about her sweaty appearance. "I should probably head out."

"Me too. Just finished my last client."

The weight room felt smaller with him in it. She gathered her things, hyperaware of his presence, the careful distance he maintained.

"I'll walk you to your car," he offered casually. "Parking lot's pretty empty this time of night."

A warning flashed in her mind. This crossed another line—small but significant. Their relationship existed within these walls, under fluorescent lights and surrounded by other people. Outside was different territory.

"I'm fine, really," she said automatically, the good-wife response ingrained after years of marriage.

"It's no trouble. I'm heading out anyway."

She hesitated, gym bag clutched in her hand. Michael was home, buried in work. The kids were doing homework or glued to their phones. No one was waiting for her immediate return. No one would notice if she took a few extra minutes.

"Okay," she heard herself say. "Thanks."

They walked through the gym's empty corridors, their footsteps echoing. At the front desk, the attendant barely looked up from her phone as they pushed through the glass doors into the night.

The parking lot was bathed in pools of yellow light from tall lamps. Her car sat alone in the far corner. She'd deliberately parked away from other vehicles—a habit from when the kids were small and she worried about door dings.

"Beautiful night," Damon commented as they walked. "Stars are out."

Erika looked up. The sky was clear, pinpricks of light visible despite the city glow. When was the last time she'd noticed the stars?

"It is," she agreed, feeling strangely light-headed. This simple walk, this small act of rebellion—choosing to spend five extra minutes with a man who wasn't her husband—sent adrenaline coursing through her.

They reached her car too quickly. She fumbled with her keys, suddenly unsure what the protocol was for ending this non-date.

"Thanks for the escort," she said, attempting lightness.

Damon nodded, but neither of them moved. The silence between them hummed with electricity.

"Erika." Her name on his lips sounded different—intimate, like a confession.

She looked up at him, her heart hammering against her ribs. "I should go."

"Should you?" His eyes held hers, giving her space to retreat, to maintain the boundary they'd been dancing around for weeks.

The question hung in the air. Should she? The correct answer was yes. The answer that clawed its way up from some buried, neglected part of her was different.

"No," she whispered.

He moved closer, still not touching her. "Tell me what you want."

The directness of his question stripped away pretense. What did she want? To feel desired. To feel alive. To reclaim some part of herself that had gone missing in the routine of her life.

"I want you to kiss me," she said, the words barely audible.

His hand came up to cup her face, thumb brushing her cheek. "Are you sure?"

She answered by rising on her toes and pressing her lips to his.

The first touch was electric. His mouth was warm, his stubble rough against her skin. He kissed her carefully at first, then with growing intensity as she responded, her gym bag dropping forgotten to the asphalt.

Erika fumbled behind her, finding the car door handle. They broke apart just long enough for her to click the unlock button on her keys. Damon opened the back door, and they tumbled inside, a tangle of limbs and urgent breath.

His weight pressed her into the leather seat, his hands exploring her body with an appreciative hunger that made her gasp. She ran her fingers through his hair, down his back, pulling him closer. His mouth moved to her neck, finding sensitive spots she'd forgotten existed.

"God, you're beautiful," he murmured against her skin.

She arched into him, years of neglect dissolving under his touch. His hand slid under her shirt, palm hot against her stomach, then higher. She moaned when he found her breast, the sound shocking in the quiet car.

Reality flickered at the edges of her consciousness—the parking lot, her wedding ring, Michael at home—but Damon's kisses pushed those thoughts away. His body between her thighs, the hardness of him evident through their clothes, sent waves of desire through her that obliterated everything else.

Damon's fingers deftly unhooked the clasp of her sports bra, freeing her breasts with a reverence that made her shiver. The cool air of the car's interior teased her skin, and her nipples hardened in anticipation. He leaned down, his breath a warm whisper against her sensitive flesh before his mouth closed over one rosy peak.

Erika's back arched off the seat as he began to nibble and suckle, each pull sending a jolt of pleasure straight to her core. Her hands roamed over the contours of his back, nails lightly scoring his skin through the fabric of his shirt.

The sensation was exquisite, overwhelming. She'd almost forgotten what it was like to be touched with such raw need, to be wanted so desperately. It was intoxicating, and she found herself craving more.

Her hand drifted down, tracing the firm length of him through his jeans. He was hard, straining against the denim, and the knowledge that she could arouse him so easily was a heady rush. She gripped him through the material, her fingers exploring his size, the shape of him.

Damon groaned against her breast, the vibration of the sound adding another layer to the symphony of sensations coursing through her. Their kisses grew deeper, more fervent, as they both sought to quench a thirst that had been building for weeks.

Erika's heart pounded in her chest, the rhythm matching the insistent throb between her legs. She could feel herself growing wet, her body preparing for him in ways that felt both foreign and exhilarating.

With a deftness that spoke of long-denied desire, Damon's hand slid down her stomach, fingers slipping beneath the waistband of her leggings. Erika's hips bucked as he found her, his touch gentle yet insistent, coaxing her toward the edge with expert precision.

They continued to explore each other, hands and mouths dancing over newly discovered landscapes, each touch stoking the flame that threatened to consume them both. The world outside the car ceased to exist; there was no past, no future—only the here and now, and the desperate need that bound them together in this moment.

Erika's mind was a whirlwind of conflicting emotions. Each touch, each kiss from Damon ignited a fire within her that she hadn't felt in years. But as his fingers worked their magic, the guilt crashed over her like a wave, dousing the flames with icy reality.

"Stop," she gasped, her voice barely above a whisper. "Please, we can't do this."

Damon lifted his head, his breath ragged. "What's wrong?"

"I... I can't." Erika's eyes brimmed with tears as she wrestled with the storm of feelings clashing inside her. "I'm married, Damon. This isn't me. It isn't who I am."

He pulled back, his expression a mix of frustration and understanding. "I get it, Erika. I do." He ran a hand through his hair, a sigh escaping him. "I crossed a line. I'm sorry. This was a mistake."

Erika fumbled to adjust her clothing, the fabric rough against her over-sensitized skin. "It's not your fault. I was a part of this too."

Damon nodded, his gaze softening as he watched her. "I shouldn't have let things go this far. You deserve better than a parking lot tryst."

She managed a weak smile. "So do you."

He reached for the door handle. "I'll give you some space."

"Damon, wait." Erika's hand shot out, catching his arm. "I don't regret it. Not really. But I can't throw away my marriage. Not like this."

"I know." He squeezed her hand reassuringly before releasing it. "Your secret's safe with me."

With that, he stepped out of the car, closing the door gently behind him. Erika watched him walk away, her heart heavy with the weight of her choices. She took a moment to collect herself, to steady her breathing, before starting the car and heading home to the life she knew—a life that now felt both familiar and irrevocably altered.

———————◆———————

Dear diary,

I've become someone I don't recognize. Tonight, in my car with Damon, I crossed a line I swore I never would. His hands on my body, his mouth on my skin... God, I can still feel him. Still smell him. Still taste him. My body hasn't felt this alive in years. When he touched me, it was like waking up from a long, dreamless sleep.

The way he looked at me—like I was beautiful, desirable, worthy of passion. Not just a mom. Not just a wife whose husband barely sees her anymore. Just a woman, wanted and craved.

But now, sitting in our dark kitchen while Michael and the kids sleep upstairs, I feel hollow. The rush is fading, leaving behind this awful, gnawing guilt. I made vows. After years of marriage, two children, a life built together. What kind of person throws that away for a few moments of pleasure in a gym parking lot?

Yet I can't stop thinking about how alive I felt. How my skin tingled under his touch. How my heart raced when he whispered my name. I've been sleepwalking through my life for so long that I forgot what it feels like to truly want and be wanted.

Michael hasn't touched me like that in years. Hasn't looked at me like I'm the center of his universe in so long I've forgotten what it feels like. When did we become strangers sharing a house? When did his work become more important than us?

I stopped myself tonight. I couldn't go through with it. But the terrifying truth is that part of me—a bigger part than I want to admit—wanted to. Wanted to feel everything Damon had to offer. Wanted to be selfish and reckless and free.

What happens now? I can't face Damon at the gym again. Can't risk falling back into that moment of weakness. But I also can't go back to being invisible in my own life.

I don't know who I am anymore. The good wife who stopped before going too far? Or the woman who betrayed her husband with her heart, if not fully with her body?

Both, I suppose. And I hate myself a little for that.

CHAPTER NINE

The Line

I lasted exactly seven days avoiding the gym. Seven days of jumping when my phone buzzed, terrified it might be Damon. Seven days of scrubbing myself raw in the shower, as if I could wash away what happened. Seven days of Michael not noticing anything different about me.

The first morning after, I woke up with my stomach in knots. I told Michael I had a stomach bug and couldn't take Lily to her soccer practice. He grumbled about rearranging his schedule but did it anyway. I spent the day cleaning obsessively, as if organizing kitchen cabinets could somehow restore order to my moral universe.

By day three, Natalie called. "Where have you been? I thought your new gym routine was non-negotiable."

"Just busy with the kids," I lied, my voice unnaturally high. I couldn't tell her. Couldn't make what happened real by speaking it aloud.

"You sound weird. Everything okay with Michael?"

I nearly broke then, nearly confessed everything. Instead, I mumbled something about PMS and changed the subject.

At dinner that night, Zach knocked over his water glass, and I snapped at him with such ferocity that everyone stared. Michael raised his eyebrows but said nothing. Later, I apologized to Zach, hugging him tight, fighting tears. My sweet boy hugged me back, completely unaware his mother was falling apart.

Day five was the worst. I found myself parked outside the gym, engine running, watching people stream in and out. I spotted Damon helping an older woman to her car, his hand on her elbow, his smile bright and attentive. Was I just another bored housewife to him? One in a long line of ego boosts? The thought made me physically ill. I drove home and took another scalding shower.

Last night, Michael reached for me in bed for the first time in weeks. I froze, guilt choking me. I pretended to be asleep until his hand retreated and his breathing deepened. Then I cried silently into my pillow.

This morning, I stared at my gym bag by the door. The membership fee automatically deducted from my account yesterday. Sixty dollars for what—to avoid the place entirely? To hide at home with my shame?

The treadmill's steady rhythm matched my heartbeat as I ran—faster than usual, sweat beading along my hairline. I'd chosen a treadmill in the corner, hoping to blend into the background. Eight o'clock on a Wednesday night meant fewer people, which was exactly what I needed.

I'd spent twenty minutes scanning the gym when I first arrived, relief washing over me when Damon was nowhere to be seen. Maybe he'd switched shifts. Maybe he'd quit. Maybe—

"Form looks good, Erika."

His voice behind me sent me lurching forward, my foot missing a step. I grabbed the handrails, recovered, and jabbed the speed down button several times.

"Sorry," Damon said, moving into view. "Didn't mean to startle you."

I kept my eyes fixed on the treadmill's digital display. "It's fine."

The silence stretched between us, filled only by the whir of my machine and the distant clang of weights.

"Haven't seen you in a while," he finally said, voice carefully neutral.

I slowed the treadmill to a walk, then stopped it completely. My legs felt suddenly unsteady. I grabbed my towel, wiped my face, buying seconds to compose myself.

"I needed some time," I said, finally looking at him.

Damon's eyes were guarded, professional. Gone was the hungry look from our last encounter. He wore the gym's standard black polo, a clipboard tucked under one arm.

"Look," I said, stepping off the treadmill. "About last time—"

"You don't need to explain."

"I do." I glanced around, lowered my voice. "I'm sorry. What happened... it shouldn't have. I'm married, and I—" My voice caught.

Damon nodded slowly. "I understand. And I crossed a line professionally."

"We both did." I twisted my wedding ring, which I'd deliberately worn tonight. "I'm not that person. I don't do things like that."

"For what it's worth," he said, his voice dropping, "I haven't stopped thinking about you."

The words hung between us, dangerous and electric. I closed my eyes briefly, fighting the pull I still felt toward him.

"I can't," I whispered. "I just can't."

The gym was near empty, the last of the evening crowd trickling out. I lingered by my car in the dimming light of the parking lot, keys clenched in my hand like a talisman. I shouldn't be here. I should be home, making dinner, helping Lily with her homework, waiting for Michael to come home from another late night at the office.

But I wasn't.

The glass doors of the gym slid open, and Damon stepped out. He paused for a moment, scanning the parking lot until his gaze landed on me. His stride was confident, purposeful as he approached.

"Erika," he said, stopping just short of me. "I thought you went home."

I shook my head, a half-hearted denial of the truth. "I don't know why I'm still here."

Damon took a step closer, his voice dropping to a murmur. "I think you do."

My breath hitched as he reached out, his fingers brushing a loose strand of hair from my face. The touch was gentle, intimate, and it sent a shiver down my spine.

"This is crazy," I said, even as my body leaned into his touch.

"Maybe," he admitted. "But it doesn't feel wrong."

I knew I should pull away, get in my car, and drive away as fast as I could. But my body seemed to have a mind of its own. My heart pounded in my chest, a rhythmic demand that I couldn't ignore.

With a shaky hand, I reached out and took his hand, intertwining my fingers with his. It was a silent surrender, an acknowledgment of the desire that I'd been fighting for weeks.

Damon's eyes darkened, and without a word, he led me around to the passenger side of my car. He opened the door, and with a last, fleeting glance at the gym's entrance, I slipped inside.

The interior of the car seemed to shrink with Damon's presence as he slid into the passenger seat. The console between us felt like a chasm, and yet, it wasn't nearly wide enough to keep us apart.

"Erika," he breathed, his hand finding my cheek. "Tell me to stop, and I will."

I closed my eyes, the taste of his name on my lips like a forbidden fruit. "Don't stop," I whispered, the words barely audible.

In the quiet of the car, with the world shut out, Damon's lips met mine in a kiss that was both a beginning and an end. It was a kiss that acknowledged the depth of the transgression we were about to commit, and yet, it was a promise of the pleasure that awaited us.

As the kiss deepened, my hands found the hem of his shirt, pulling it up, needing to feel the warmth of his skin against my palms. His muscles tensed under my touch, a silent testament to his own restraint.

With fumbling hands, I undid his belt, the metallic rasp of the buckle loud in the confined space. My heart was a drumbeat in my ears, a primal rhythm that drowned out any lingering doubts.

Damon's breath hitched as I slid down the seat, my movements guided by an instinct that felt as old as time. My fingers trembled as I freed him from his clothes, my gaze locked with his as I took him into my mouth.

The taste of him, the heat, the power I held in that moment—it was intoxicating. I felt him shudder, heard the sharp intake of his breath, and it fueled my own desire.

This was uncharted territory, a landscape I'd never explored. And yet, it felt like a homecoming, a reclaiming of a part of myself that I thought I'd lost.

As I moved over him, my world narrowed to the feel of him against my tongue, the ragged cadence of his breathing, and the silent promise that this was only the beginning.

The world outside the car receded to a distant murmur as I explored him with a hunger I hadn't known I possessed. Damon's fingers threaded through my hair, a gentle anchor as I moved with a rhythm that was both new and exhilarating.

My tongue traced the length of him, learning the contours, the textures, the places that made his breath catch and his body tense. I watched his face, the way his eyes darkened to near blackness, the way his lips parted on a silent moan.

The scent of him filled my senses—clean sweat mingling with the musk of arousal. It was a potent combination, one that sparked a corresponding heat within me, an ache that demanded satisfaction.

Damon's hands tightened in my hair, his body coiling like a spring. "Erika," he groaned, the sound a plea and a warning all at once.

I didn't pull away. Instead, I redoubled my efforts, driven by a primal need to bring him to the edge and watch him fall. My hand joined my mouth, working in tandem as I took him deeper, faster, my own body throbbing in time with his escalating need.

His body went rigid, a low growl escaping his lips as he reached his climax. There was a moment of stillness, a breath held in anticipation, and then he was spilling into my mouth, the salty tang of him shocking and intimate.

I swallowed reflexively, my eyes locked on his as he came undone. Wave after wave of release shook him, and I rode it out, my hand slowing but not stopping until his body finally relaxed, the tension flowing out of him in a long, shuddering sigh.

For a moment, neither of us moved. The only sounds were our mingled breathing and the distant hum of the city at night. The intimacy of the act settled over us like a blanket, warm and heavy.

Damon's hand cupped my cheek, his thumb brushing across my lips in a silent gesture of awe and gratitude. "You are incredible," he whispered, his voice rough with emotion.

I sat up, wiping the corner of my mouth with the back of my hand, a sense of empowerment surging through me. I had done this. I had taken control in a way I never had before. And it felt incredible.

The weight of what we'd done hung in the air between us, a silent acknowledgment that things had irrevocably changed. There was no going back to the way things were before, no pretending that the boundaries we'd crossed could be un-crossed.

The steering wheel felt cold beneath my trembling fingers as I pulled out of the gym parking lot. Tears blurred the streetlights into hazy stars, forcing me to swipe at my eyes every few seconds just to see the road ahead.

My lips still tingled from Damon's kisses. The taste of him lingered in my mouth. Evidence of what we'd done.

"What have I done?" I whispered to the empty car. My voice sounded foreign to my ears, ragged and broken.

A sob escaped me at the red light, and I covered my mouth to stifle the sound. The woman in the car next to mine glanced over, her face a mask of concern. I turned away, unable to bear even a stranger's gaze.

I'd crossed a line tonight. One I'd never thought I would. Fifteen years of marriage, thrown into question by twenty minutes in a parked car.

The light changed, and I accelerated too quickly, the engine protesting with a whine. My body still hummed with electricity, with the thrill of Damon's touch, his words, the way he'd looked at me. The way he'd wanted me.

The guilt crashed over me in waves, threatening to drown me. And yet beneath it ran an undercurrent of something else. Something I was ashamed to acknowledge.

Excitement.

My phone buzzed in my purse. Michael. I couldn't answer. Not now. Not with the evidence of my betrayal so fresh.

I pulled into our driveway, killed the engine, and sat in darkness. Our house loomed before me, windows glowing with warm light. Inside were my children. My husband. My life.

But something else had awakened in me tonight. Something hungry and reckless that had been dormant for too long.

I pressed my forehead against the steering wheel and let the tears come freely. Guilt and excitement warred within me, neither willing to concede.

What terrified me most wasn't what I'd done with Damon.

It was how badly I wanted to do it again.

CHAPTER TEN

Confession

The coffee shop buzzed with mid-morning energy as I slid into the booth across from Natalie. She'd already ordered my usual—a vanilla latte with an extra shot.

"You look like hell," Natalie said, pushing the mug toward me.

I wrapped my hands around the warm ceramic. "Thanks. Just what every woman wants to hear."

"What's going on? You sounded weird on the phone." Her eyes narrowed. "And you're doing that thing with your hair."

I dropped the strand I'd been twisting. "What thing?"

"The nervous twirling thing. You've done it since college." She leaned forward. "Spill it."

My throat tightened. I'd rehearsed this conversation a dozen times on the drive over, but now the words stuck like glue.

"I did something." The confession came out as a whisper.

Natalie's eyebrows shot up. "Something as in...?"

"Remember that trainer I told you about?" Heat rushed to my face. "We... I..."

"Holy shit." Natalie's eyes widened. "You and the hot trainer?"

I nodded, staring into my untouched coffee.

"How far did it go?" Her voice dropped to a conspiratorial whisper.

"Not all the way, but... far enough." The memory flashed through my mind—his hands, his mouth, the way I'd responded. "Far enough that I can't pretend it didn't happen."

Natalie reached across the table and squeezed my hand. "How do you feel?"

"Terrible. Exhilarated. Confused." I finally met her eyes. "I never thought I'd be this person, Nat. The cheating wife. That's not me."

"Hey, you're not defined by one mistake."

"That's just it." I swallowed hard. "It didn't feel like a mistake when it was happening. It felt... necessary. Like I could finally breathe again."

Natalie studied me for a long moment. "And Michael still has no idea?"

"How could he? He barely looks at me anymore." The bitterness in my voice surprised even me.

"What are you going to do now?"

I shook my head. "I don't know. Part of me wants to confess everything and beg forgiveness. And part of me..."

"Wants to see the trainer again," she finished for me.

I couldn't bring myself to confirm it out loud, but my silence was answer enough.

Natalie's eyes widened. "Erika Lawrence, stop being vague. What exactly happened between you two?"

I glanced around the coffee shop, lowering my voice to barely above a whisper. "I went down on him, okay? In my car. In the gym parking lot."

"You gave him a—" Natalie caught herself, leaning closer. "In your car? Where anyone could see?"

I covered my face with my hands. "We were in the back corner of the lot. It was dark."

"I didn't even know you had it in you." Natalie looked impressed rather than judgmental. "Was it... good?"

The memory rushed back—his fingers tangled in my hair, the sounds he made, the heady power I felt.

"It was... incredible." My voice sounded different, even to my own ears. "I haven't felt that way in years. Maybe ever."

"Better than with Michael?"

I nodded, shame and excitement battling within me. "So much better. He was so responsive, so appreciative." I traced the rim of my coffee mug. "He made me feel like I was doing something amazing, not just... fulfilling an obligation."

"And now?"

"Now I can't stop thinking about it. About him." I met Natalie's gaze directly. "I want to see him again. I want to do more. Everything, actually."

"You mean..."

"Yes. I want to sleep with him." Saying it out loud sent a shiver through me. "Is that terrible? That makes me terrible, right?"

"It makes you human," Natalie said softly. "Look, I'm not going to sit here and tell you cheating is great. But I understand wanting to feel desired again. You have needs. It's not as if you haven't tried to get Michael to satisfy them, but he's turned you down time and time again. So I certainly get why you did it."

"It's not just about being desired." I struggled to articulate the feeling. "It's about feeling alive. When I was with him, I wasn't just someone's wife or someone's mother. I was just... me. A woman with desires and needs."

Natalie took a sip of her coffee, considering my words. "You know what? I think I understand better than most people would."

"You do?"

"Remember when I first got divorced? Everyone treated me like I was broken. Like I'd failed at the most basic thing a woman should succeed at." She rolled her eyes. "But you know what I discovered?"

I shook my head.

"Freedom. The chance to figure out who I am when I'm not trying to be what someone else needs me to be." She leaned forward. "Maybe this isn't just about sex. Maybe it's about re-discovering yourself."

The knot in my chest loosened slightly. "I didn't expect you to understand."

"Why? Because good girls don't cheat?" Natalie laughed softly. "Life's complicated, Erika. We're all just doing our best."

"But my family—"

"Will be fine. This doesn't have to be about them. This can be just for you." She reached across and squeezed my hand. "When was the last time you did something just for yourself?"

I tried to remember. "I... can't remember."

"Exactly." Natalie's expression softened. "Look, I'm not saying blow up your marriage. I'm just saying maybe you deserve to explore this part of yourself. The part that's been suffocating for years."

"You don't think I'm horrible?"

"I think you're human. And I think you've spent fifteen years putting everyone else first." She smiled. "Maybe it's time to put yourself first for once."

Something shifted inside me—a weight lifting, a door opening. For the first time since that night in the car, I felt something other than guilt. I felt possibility.

"So what now?" I asked.

"That's entirely up to you." Natalie's eyes sparkled with mischief. "But if you're asking for my opinion, I say see where this goes. Safely, discreetly, but... see where it goes."

"And if it's just physical?"

"Then enjoy it for what it is." She shrugged. "Not everything needs to be forever."

I toyed with my empty mug, considering Natalie's words. The weight of her permission—or at least her understanding—settled over me like a warm blanket.

"You know," Natalie said, lowering her voice, "if you're serious about exploring this side of yourself, the gym might not be the smartest place."

I frowned. "What do you mean?"

"Think about it. You go there regularly. People know you. Your trainer works there." She ticked off points on her fingers. "If things go south, or if someone recognizes you, that's your daily routine compromised."

My stomach tightened. "I hadn't thought of that."

"Plus, workplace hookups get messy. Trust me." She grimaced. "What if he gets possessive? Or starts expecting more? You'd have nowhere to escape."

"So what are you suggesting?"

Natalie glanced around before leaning closer. "If you want to experiment, maybe consider something more... anonymous."

"Anonymous?" The word felt dangerous on my tongue.

"There are apps, websites. Places where people looking for no-strings encounters can connect." She shrugged. "No history, no mutual friends, no awkward run-ins at the grocery store."

"You mean like... hookup apps?" The concept seemed alien, something from another woman's life.

"Exactly. You control everything—who you talk to, what information you share, where you meet." She took a sip of her coffee. "And when you're done, you walk away. Clean break."

"That sounds so calculated." I twisted my wedding ring unconsciously.

"It's practical. And safer, in a way." Natalie's expression grew serious. "Look, what happened with your trainer was spontaneous and exciting. But if you're thinking of doing this again, being strategic might protect you—and your family—from unnecessary complications."

The idea settled over me, strange yet oddly compelling. A controlled environment for the most uncontrolled feelings I'd had in years.

"I wouldn't even know where to start," I admitted.

"Start with a separate email account. Then a profile with limited personal details." She smiled sympathetically. "You don't have to decide right now. Just something to consider."

"And you think that's... better somehow?"

"I think it's more contained. The gym trainer knows where you live, knows your name, could potentially run into your kids someday." Natalie's pragmatism cut through my romantic notions. "Anonymous encounters stay anonymous. That's the whole point."

CHAPTER ELEVEN

Digital Hunting Ground

Three days passed. Natalie's words echoed in my head while I packed lunches, helped with homework, and smiled through Michael's distracted kisses goodbye. The idea she'd planted grew like a seed in fertile soil, taking root deeper with each passing hour.

Thursday afternoon, the house fell silent. Michael at work, Zach at baseball practice, Lily at her friend's until dinner. Three hours of solitude stretched before me.

I poured a glass of wine, though it wasn't even two o'clock. My hands trembled slightly as I opened my laptop at the kitchen table.

"This is insane," I whispered to the empty room.

I created a new Gmail account—something generic with random numbers that couldn't be traced back to me. No personal information, nothing connected to my real life.

The dating app Natalie had mentioned took less than five minutes to download. Each field in the profile form made my heart beat faster. Age: 35. Status: It didn't have "married but looking" as an option, so I selected "It's complicated." Location: I chose a neighborhood twenty minutes away.

For the photos, I scrolled through my phone. Most pictures showed me with family or friends—too recognizable. Finally, I found one from Natalie's birthday last year. Me in dim lighting, laughing, head tilted back. I cropped it just below my eyes, showing only my smile, neck, and shoulders. Anonymous yet inviting.

The bio was hardest. What exactly was I looking for? What could I admit to wanting? After several attempts, I settled on something simple: "Looking for uncomplicated connection. Intelligent conversation and chemistry a must. Not interested in forever, just the present moment."

My finger hovered over the "Create Profile" button for a full minute before I finally pressed it. The screen refreshed, showing my new digital persona to the world.

"What am I doing?" I whispered, taking a long sip of wine.

I scrolled through a few profiles of men in my area, my face burning with each swipe. Some looked like corporate types, others more casual. All seeking something outside their normal lives, just like me.

Setting the phone down, I leaned back in my chair and waited, caught between the urge to delete everything and the thrill of anticipation of the first notification appearing.

Within an hour, my phone wouldn't stop buzzing. Ten notifications, then twenty, then more than I could count. Each vibration sent a jolt through my body—equal parts excitement and dread.

I hadn't expected this level of attention. These weren't just casual hellos. Men had written thoughtful messages, asked specific questions about my vague profile, sent compliments that made my cheeks flush. Some were crude, easily deleted, but many seemed genuinely interested in the mysterious woman I'd presented.

"Jesus," I muttered, scrolling through the endless stream. My wine glass sat empty beside me.

One message caught my eye from a man called David—professional-looking, early forties, with kind eyes and a profile that mentioned he traveled often for business. "I appreciate your honesty," he'd written. "Seems we might be looking for similar things. Coffee sometime?"

My fingers hovered over the keyboard. This was real now. Not just a fantasy or a late-night conversation with Natalie. Actual men wanted to meet me—the real me, not just the mother and wife I'd become.

I set the phone down and paced the kitchen. What had started as a curious exploration suddenly felt overwhelming. These weren't just digital profiles; they were real people with expectations, desires, and lives as complicated as mine.

"This is too much," I whispered to myself, glancing at the family calendar on the refrigerator. Soccer practice. Dentist appointments. Anniversary dinner next month. The reality of my life stared back at me while my phone continued to buzz with possibilities of a different one.

I returned to the table and picked up my phone, my hand trembling slightly. The notifications had doubled. Men of all types waiting for my response, each representing a potential path away from the loneliness I'd been feeling, each carrying risks I couldn't fully calculate.

Dear diary,

I've crossed a line today. Created a profile. Set something in motion that I can't fully control. The responses came flooding in—so many men, all wanting something from the woman in that cropped photo. It's both terrifying and intoxicating.

I need rules. Boundaries. If I'm really going to do this (am I?), I can't just stumble blindly forward.

My criteria for whoever I might actually meet:

I've narrowed it down to three possibilities. David seems the most promising—business consultant, travels weekly, thoughtful messages. There's also Thomas, an architect who works primarily in the city, and Christopher, who seems intelligent but maybe a bit too eager.

Michael didn't even notice when I came to bed last night. Just rolled over and continued sleeping. How did we get here? When did I become invisible to him?

This isn't who I thought I'd be at 35. The woman with the secret profile, contemplating meeting strangers. But I don't recognize the woman in my mirror anymore either.

Tomorrow I'll respond to David. Just coffee. Just conversation. I can always walk away.

CHAPTER TWELVE

The Hotel Bar

"A regional bookkeeping conference?" Michael glanced up from his laptop, his eyes meeting mine for perhaps the first time in days.

"Yeah, it's in Portland. Friday through Sunday." I kept my voice casual while folding laundry, grateful I'd researched actual conferences before mentioning it. "The firm is covering the hotel, and I'd only need to pay for meals. They're offering certification credits."

"This weekend?"

"Next weekend." I placed his neatly folded shirts in the basket. "I've been handling the Peterson account solo for months now. The advanced QuickBooks sessions would really help streamline things."

Michael returned to his screen, the blue light reflecting off his glasses. "Makes sense. The kids have that thing Saturday anyway."

"Zach's debate tournament. I already talked to him about it. He understands." I paused, waiting for questions that didn't come. "Lily's sleeping at Emma's that night, so you'd just need to take Zach."

"Sure." His fingers resumed their typing.

The ease of his agreement should have been a relief. Instead, it stung. No questions about which hotel, no disappointment about missing a weekend together, not even mild curiosity about the conference schedule.

Later that night, I booked a room at the Riverside Hotel—not the conference hotel I'd mentioned to Michael, but one across town, where I'd be less likely to run into anyone who might actually be attending the fabricated event. I confirmed my meeting with David for Saturday afternoon. Just coffee, I reminded myself. Just conversation.

I created a fake conference schedule on my laptop, complete with session descriptions and speaker bios pulled from similar events. I even printed a name badge and registration confirmation. The thoroughness of my deception surprised me—these weren't the actions of someone "just testing the waters" or "just having coffee."

In my closet, I selected outfits nothing like what I'd wear to an actual conference—a dress I'd bought years ago but never had occasion to wear, heels higher than I'd worn since before the kids were born, lingerie still with tags attached.

"Just in case," I whispered to my reflection, not wanting to name what the "case" might be.

———◆◇◆———

The Riverside Hotel's bar glowed with amber light that flattered everyone beneath it. I'd arrived twenty minutes early, claiming a corner table with a view of both entrances. My third glass of pinot noir sat half-finished before me—liquid courage that wasn't quite working.

I wore the dress I'd packed—navy blue with a neckline that dipped just low enough to be interesting without screaming desperation. My wedding ring rested in a zippered pocket of my purse.

At precisely seven, he walked in. David was exactly as his photos promised—tall with salt-and-pepper hair, wearing a charcoal suit that suggested business meetings earlier in the day. His profile had said 42, divorced, financial advisor. His messages had been witty, respectful, and just suggestive enough to make my pulse quicken.

He scanned the room, and I raised my hand in a small wave. Recognition flashed across his face, followed by an appreciative smile that made my cheeks warm.

"Erika?" He approached my table. "Even more beautiful than your pictures."

"That's quite the line." I smiled despite myself. "Does it usually work?"

"I wouldn't know. This is actually my first time doing.. . whatever this is." He gestured between us with a self-deprecating laugh. "Mind if I sit?"

I nodded toward the chair across from mine. "How do I know that's not a line too?"

"Fair question." He settled into the seat, loosening his tie slightly. "I've been divorced for eleven months. My sister set up my profile. I've had exactly three conversations before yours, and you're the first person I've met in person."

The bartender approached, and David ordered a scotch, neat.

"So why me?" I asked when we were alone again.

"Your smile." He leaned forward. "In that one clear photo, you had the most beautiful smile, yet there was also a sense of sadness behind it. I don't know, maybe I'm way off base but at least that's the sense I got." He paused. "Also, you didn't have any inspirational quotes in your profile, which was refreshing."

I laughed, genuine and unexpected. "Low bar."

"You'd be surprised." His drink arrived, and he raised it slightly. "To first meetings."

I clinked my glass against his. "To first meetings."

The first drink melted into a second. David's posture loosened, and the professional veneer slipped away. We'd exhausted small talk about the hotel, the weather, our fictitious conference and business trip.

"So," I set my glass down firmly. "We should probably address why we're really here."

David nodded, his eyes meeting mine with surprising directness. "Probably should."

"What are you looking for, David? Really?"

He traced the rim of his glass, considering. "Honestly? Connection without complication." He looked up. "My marriage was seventeen years of emotional warfare disguised as partnership. The divorce was brutal. I'm not ready for anything serious, but I miss..." He paused. "I miss being touched. Being wanted."

"And that's it?" I pressed.

"No expectations beyond tonight. No promises I can't keep. Just two adults enjoying each other's company." He leaned forward. "What about you? What brought you here?"

The question hung between us. I'd rehearsed various lies, but something in his candor made me braver than intended.

"I'm married."

His expression didn't change. "I figured."

"You did?"

"The tan line on your finger. The way you keep touching where your ring should be."

I took a deep breath. "My husband hasn't really seen me in years. Not in any way that matters." The words tumbled out faster now. "I have this life that looks perfect from the outside. Mother, wife, part-time bookkeeper. But inside I'm... disappearing."

"And what do you want tonight?"

"To feel something. To be desired. To remember what it's like when someone looks at you and actually wants you." I swallowed hard. "No strings, no drama. Just... presence. Attention. The opposite of what I have at home."

David nodded slowly. "And after tonight?"

"We go back to our separate lives. This stays here."

"And you're sure about this? No regrets tomorrow?"

I thought about Michael's back turned to me in bed, about the hollow feeling in my chest each time he worked late, about the countless nights I'd cried silently in the bathroom.

"The only thing I regret is waiting this long to feel alive again."

David finished his scotch and set the glass down with quiet deliberation. His eyes never left mine.

"So where do you want to go from here?"

The directness of his question caught me off guard. In my fantasies, this moment had played out differently—the man taking charge, making decisions, sweeping me along in a current I could pretend not to control. But David wasn't playing that game. He was putting the choice squarely in my hands.

I twisted the stem of my wineglass, watching the burgundy liquid catch the light. The background noise of the bar seemed to fade as I weighed what I truly wanted. The familiar guilt churned in my stomach, but alongside it was something stronger—a hunger I'd denied for too long.

"I..." My voice faltered. I cleared my throat and tried again, meeting his gaze. "I think we should explore our desires."

The words hung between us, impossibly bold in the dim light. I couldn't believe they'd come from my mouth—proper Erika, reliable Erika, mother-of-two Erika. But they had, and I didn't want to take them back.

David's expression softened. He reached across the table, his fingers brushing against mine. The simple contact sent electricity up my arm.

"Are you certain?" His voice was low, serious. "Once we leave this bar together..."

"I know what I'm doing." The conviction in my voice surprised even me. "I've thought about this—about something like this—for longer than I care to admit."

He nodded, a small smile playing at the corners of his mouth. "Then let me get the check."

As David signaled for the bartender, I felt a curious lightness. The weight of should-nots and what-ifs that had burdened me for years seemed to lift, replaced by a thrilling vertigo of possibility. For the first time in so long, I wasn't thinking about tomorrow's carpools or Michael's schedule or the grocery list. I was simply present, awake to the moment and my own desires.

———— ◆○◆ ————

The hotel room was a blank canvas, a temporary escape from the life painted in shades of beige and routine. David closed the door behind us, the click of the latch a soundless echo of finality. This was it—the point of no return.

I stood by the window, looking out at the city lights, feeling the thrum of the unknown pulse through me. David approached from behind, his hands resting gently on my shoulders. The touch was tentative, questioning, as though he expected me to bolt at any second. But I didn't. Instead, I leaned back into him, feeling the solid warmth of another body against mine.

Slowly, his fingers traced the line of my jaw, tilting my face up toward his. Our lips met in a kiss that was hesitant at first, then deepened with a mix of urgency and relief. It was a stark contrast to the perfunctory pecks I'd grown accustomed to, each movement deliberate and charged with a palpable need.

David's hands moved with a practiced ease, unbuttoning my blouse, peeling away the layers that I had used to shield myself from the world. My skin tingled at the exposure, a flush creeping across my chest as he drank in the sight of me.

We moved to the bed, a tangle of limbs and eager hands. My body responded with a fervor I hadn't known in years, every nerve alight with the newness of his touch. He explored me with a reverence that made me feel cherished, worshipped, and for a moment, I allowed myself to believe that this—this fire and passion and desire—was something I deserved.

As we undressed each other, the air was thick with the scent of our longing. His mouth found the sensitive spots I'd nearly forgotten—the curve of my neck, the hollow at the base of my throat, the peaks of my breasts. Each kiss, each caress, was a whisper against the silence I'd been living in.

When he entered me, it was with a sweetness that brought tears to my eyes. This was sex, yes, but it was also a homecoming, a reclaiming of a part of myself that I'd locked away. With each thrust, I felt more alive, more present, more powerful.

The climax hit me with an intensity that was both familiar and completely new. It was a wave that crashed over me, again and again, obliterating everything but the feeling of David's body moving against mine.

Afterward, we lay in the tangle of sheets, our breathing slowly returning to normal. I listened to the steady beat of his heart beneath my ear, a rhythm that felt like a secret language between us.

The room was quiet, save for the soft hum of the city outside. I could feel the weight of the decision I'd made, the enormity of crossing a line I'd never thought I would. There was no turning back now, no pretending that this night hadn't changed me.

I extricated myself from David's embrace and padded silently to the bathroom. I caught sight of my reflection in the mirror, my cheeks flushed, my lips swollen from his kisses. I looked alive—wild, even. The woman staring back at me was a stranger, and yet, she was more truly me than I'd been in years.

I reached for my diary, tucked away in my purse. The pen felt heavy in my hand as I considered what to write. This was a moment that demanded documentation, a memory to be captured in all its raw, unvarnished truth.

I began to write, the words flowing with an ease that surprised me. I didn't shy away from the details—the taste of his skin, the pressure of his hands, the sound of my own moans filling the room. It was explicit, yes, but it was also a testament to a desire that refused to be ignored any longer.

As I closed the diary and slipped back into bed beside David, I knew that this encounter would be etched into my soul forever. It wasn't just about the sex; it was about rediscovering a part of myself that I'd thought was lost.

And in the quiet of that hotel room, with the echoes of our passion still lingering in the air, I allowed myself to bask in the afterglow of a desire finally fulfilled.

CHAPTER THIRTEEN

The Rush

The alarm blared at six, jolting me from dreams of hotel sheets and unfamiliar hands. I silenced it with a slap and stared at the ceiling, Michael's steady breathing beside me a reminder of reality.

I slipped from bed without waking him and padded to the kitchen. The coffee maker gurgled to life as I leaned against the counter, my mind drifting back to David's hotel room. Three days had passed since my "conference," yet the memory remained electric against the backdrop of my routine.

"Mom, where's my history textbook?" Zach thundered down the stairs, backpack half-zipped.

I pointed to the dining table. "Right where you left it yesterday."

Lily appeared next, complaining about the Wi-Fi speed while scrolling through her phone. The morning chaos unfolded with mechanical precision – lunches packed, permission slips signed, Michael kissing my cheek before rushing out the door.

At work, I stared at spreadsheets until the numbers blurred. The fluorescent lights hummed overhead, casting everything in a flat, unforgiving glow. My coworker droned about her weekend gardening project while I nodded at appropriate intervals, my thoughts elsewhere.

That evening, I stood at the stove stirring spaghetti sauce. The rhythmic motion felt like a prison sentence. The sauce bubbled. The pasta boiled. The garlic bread browned. The same meals, the same plates, the same table conversation about teachers and homework and office politics.

After dinner, Michael flipped through channels before settling on a home renovation show we'd seen twice before. I sat beside him, book open in my lap, reading the same paragraph four times without absorbing a word.

"You've been quiet," he said during a commercial, his eyes still on the screen.

"Just tired," I replied, the lie coming easily.

In bed that night, I scrolled through my phone, finger hovering over the dating app. The notifications had piled up – men waiting for responses, new matches accumulating. Each one represented a doorway to something vivid and alive, while around me, my actual life had faded to grayscale.

I set my phone aside and stared into the darkness. The ceiling fan turned lazy circles above me. Michael's breathing deepened into sleep. The house creaked and settled.

Everything was exactly as it had always been, and suddenly, that felt unbearable.

I started checking the app first thing in the morning, before even getting out of bed. The soft blue glow illuminated my face in the pre-dawn darkness while Michael slept beside me. My thumb moved with practiced precision—swipe, pause, consider, match.

During lunch breaks, I'd slip away to my car, not to eat but to scroll through messages. The heat of anticipation replaced hunger as I crafted responses, each word carefully chosen to maintain the version of myself I'd created—confident, carefree, unburdened.

"We could meet at that new hotel downtown," wrote one man, his profile showing just enough of his face to reveal a strong jawline and the hint of a smile.

In my mind, I was already there—stepping into a sleek lobby, elevator doors closing behind us, his hand on the small of my back. I imagined the way he might kiss, whether he'd be gentle at first or immediately commanding. Would he want to talk afterward or simply leave? Each possibility created its own branch of scenarios, a sprawling tree of alternate lives I could step into and out of at will.

Traffic lights became opportunities to check notifications. School pickup lines transformed into stolen moments to reply to messages. Even dinner prep wasn't safe—I'd prop my phone against the spice rack, angle it away from the doorway, and switch screens whenever I heard footsteps.

"Earth to Erika," Michael waved his hand in front of my face one evening as I stirred pasta, my mind lost in a conversation with a lawyer from Scottsdale.

"Sorry, just thinking about work stuff," I murmured, pocketing my phone.

During Lily's dance recital, I excused myself twice to use the restroom, each time locking myself in a stall to respond to a particularly intriguing message. Standing before the mirror afterward, I barely recognized the woman who adjusted her blouse and reapplied lipstick, eyes bright with secrets.

The app became a phantom limb—even when I wasn't actively using it, I felt its presence, the weight of possibilities in my pocket. My thoughts wandered to it during PTA meetings, during conversations with my children.

"Mom, did you hear anything I just said?" Zach's voice cut through my mental fog.

I blinked, lowering my phone beneath the kitchen counter. "Of course, honey. Something about... your science project?"

"My history presentation. It's tomorrow and I needed you to look over it." His eyes narrowed. "You promised last night."

The guilt hit like a physical blow. I had promised—vaguely remembered nodding while typing a message to the architect from Phoenix who wanted to meet for drinks.

"I'm sorry, let me see it now." I reached for his laptop, but the damage was done. Zach's shoulders slumped as he slid it toward me.

"Never mind. Dad already helped me."

My boss's voice echoed in my head from earlier that day: "Erika, this is the second time this month the Donaldson account numbers don't match. Are you feeling alright?"

I wasn't. The numbers swam before my eyes as notifications kept pulling my attention away. I'd started making careless errors, forgetting to enter data, double-booking client meetings. Things I'd never done before.

One Tuesday, I completely forgot to pick up Lily from volleyball practice. She called after waiting forty minutes, her voice small and confused. "Did something happen? Are you okay?"

I raced to the school, heart hammering, finding her sitting alone on the curb, knees pulled to her chest. The coach had already left.

"I'm so sorry, sweetie. I got caught up with..." I couldn't even fabricate a believable excuse.

That night, I found myself sitting in the car in our garage, scrolling through messages for twenty minutes before going inside. Michael had already made dinner. The kids were quiet, exchanging looks I pretended not to see.

Later, I locked myself in the bathroom, perched on the edge of the tub, and arranged to meet a corporate lawyer the following weekend. My hands shook as I typed. This wasn't excitement anymore—it was something else, something that felt less like choice and more like compulsion.

CHAPTER FOURTEEN

Expanding Parameters

I expanded my search radius, then adjusted my age preferences. Thirty to fifty-five became twenty-five to sixty. The app refreshed, delivering a flood of new faces.

My thumb hovered over the profile of a twenty-eight-year-old tattoo artist with gauged ears and a neck tattoo. Nothing like Michael's clean-cut banker aesthetic. Nothing like the businessmen I'd been meeting. My finger tapped the screen before I could reconsider.

Later that night, I created a new folder on my phone labeled "Budget Templates" and filled it with screenshots of men who represented something different—a musician with long hair and calloused fingers, a blue-collar construction worker with sun-weathered skin, a soft-spoken literature professor with wire-rimmed glasses.

"You're going after types now?" Natalie asked over coffee, eyebrow raised as I showed her my collection.

"I'm conducting research." I stirred my latte, avoiding her eyes. "Different experiences. Different... techniques."

She laughed. "Like you're collecting Pokémon?"

I didn't laugh. Something about her description felt uncomfortably accurate.

That weekend, I met the tattoo artist at a dive bar I'd never have entered six months ago. His hands were nothing like the manicured fingers of the businessmen I'd been with—they were stained with ink, nails cut short, knuckles adorned with faded blue symbols. When he touched me later in his studio apartment, the callouses on his fingertips created friction I'd never felt before.

The following Tuesday, it was the silver-haired investment banker in his fifties, old enough to be calculating retirement options. His downtown condo overlooked the city, and he poured aged whiskey into crystal tumblers before we even spoke about why I was there.

Thursday afternoon, I claimed a dentist appointment to meet the grad student who lived in a cramped apartment filled with books and vinyl records. He approached sex with the same earnest enthusiasm he probably brought to his dissertation.

I created a spreadsheet—not of names, never names—but of types, experiences, sensations. The yoga instructor who bent me into positions I didn't know were possible. The ex-military man whose discipline extended to every aspect of the encounter. The shy IT specialist whose awkwardness vanished in private.

Each meeting filled a slot in my taxonomy of desire. Each man became a category rather than a person.

I labeled the prepaid Visa card "Emergency Funds" in my wallet, tucked behind my regular credit cards where Michael would never look. The activation receipt went through the shredder. The pin—Zach's original due date, not his actual birthday—something only I would remember.

"I need to organize the family finances better," I told Michael over breakfast, not meeting his eyes. "I'm creating separate accounts for different expenses."

He nodded absently, scrolling through emails on his phone. "Whatever makes sense to you, honey."

My new system took shape with frightening efficiency. I volunteered for the PTA fundraising committee—perfect cover for evening meetings that never happened. I created a digital calendar with color-coded appointments that synced to our family account: blue for real events, red for my fabricated ones.

"Mom's really getting involved this year," I overheard Lily tell her father one evening.

"Book club every other Thursday," I announced casually at dinner. "We're reading contemporary fiction." In reality, I'd created a dummy Gmail account where I saved PDFs of book summaries—enough to discuss the plot if questioned. I even highlighted passages and made margin notes.

The bookkeeping clients I claimed to visit never existed. The invoices I created—complete with letterhead and tax ID numbers—went into a password-protected folder on my laptop. The money I supposedly earned went straight to my secret fund.

I bought a second phone—a basic model with prepaid minutes. The contacts were saved under innocuous names: "Dentist Office," "Hair Salon," "Gym Membership." I kept it charged in my glove compartment, only powering it on when I was alone.

For overnight trips, I photographed myself in hotel conference rooms during legitimate daytime events, creating visual evidence of professional development workshops I never attended. I collected name badges, promotional pens, and program booklets as props.

"You seem more organized lately," Natalie observed as I declined a lunch invitation, consulting my fabricated schedule.

"Just trying to keep everything straight," I replied, wondering when lying had become so effortless.

Dear diary,

The wind outside my window is relentless tonight, howling like a wolf in the dark. It's fitting, really, for the thoughts that are prowling around in my head, wild and untamed.

I've started a list—a sexual "bucket list," if you will. It's a catalog of desires I've harbored, fantasies I've brushed against in the quiet hours of the night but never dared to touch in the light of day. Never with Michael.

I've written these desires in the pages of my diary, beneath the veneer of mundane entries about grocery lists and parent-teacher conferences. Each word is a heartbeat, a pulse of longing that throbs with the possibility of what could be.

When I close the diary, my hands are shaking. I am both terrified and exhilarated by the woman I see reflected in these words—a woman I am only just beginning to discover.

CHAPTER FIFTEEN

The Afternoon Men

Erika's diary lay open on her desk, the ink of her confessions still glistening wet. The house was quiet, the teens at school and Michael absorbed in his work. She stared at the list she'd made, her heart pounding with a mixture of fear and excitement. It was one thing to fantasize, quite another to act.

The clock on the wall ticked away the minutes, a relentless reminder that life was passing her by. She looked at her calendar, filled with the mundane: doctor's appointments, school plays, work schedules. But there, nestled between a dentist appointment and a parent-teacher conference, was an opening. A two-hour window that could be her escape hatch.

Erika reached for her phone, her hands trembling. She opened the dating app, her profile picture a tantalizing mix of mystery and allure. The messages poured in, a stream of possibilities. She sifted through them, searching for a match that could fit into her constrained schedule.

There he was—a man who introduced himself as Alex. A lawyer, with an office in the heart of the city. His messages were confident, direct. He suggested they meet for a quick lunch, his words laced with an undertone of desire that left little to the imagination.

Erika felt a surge of adrenaline. She typed out her response, her fingers flying over the keys. "Lunch sounds perfect," she said, the lie slipping easily from her tongue. She would tell her boss she needed to run an errand, that she'd be back before anyone noticed she was gone.

The day of the rendezvous arrived, and Erika found herself stepping into an elevator, her heart racing as she ascended to the floor where Alex's office was located. She wore a dress that clung to her curves, her hair styled in soft waves. She felt beautiful, desirable—a far cry from the invisible woman she'd become at home.

The doors dinged open, and there he was, waiting for her. Alex was everything his profile had promised: tall, with a commanding presence and eyes that promised wicked things. He greeted her with a kiss on the cheek, his hand lingering at the small of her back as he led her into his office.

They barely made it to the couch before their lips met, the urgency of their need for one another making a mockery of the word "lunch." Erika found herself lost in the moment, the world outside the tinted windows of the high-rise fading into insignificance.

Erika's breath hitched as Alex's hands roamed over her body, exploring the contours of her hips, her thighs, with an urgency that left her dizzy. His touch was both a question and a demand, a silent inquiry that sought permission even as it took what it wanted.

They moved together as one, each touch, each kiss, a step towards a precipice that Erika had never dared approach before. The fabric of her dress bunched up around her waist, a testament to the frenzy of their desire. Alex's fingers traced the lacy edge of her underwear, a whisper of a touch that sent shivers up her spine.

With a deftness that spoke of experience, he unhooked her bra, his eyes darkening as her breasts spilled into his waiting hands. He took her nipples between his fingers, rolling them until they were hard peaks, a moan escaping her lips as he bent his head to take one into his mouth.

Erika's hands found the zipper of his trousers, her fingers fumbling in her haste to feel him, to hold him. He was hard and ready, and the knowledge that she had this effect on him sent a thrill of power coursing through her veins.

Alex's breath was hot against her ear as he whispered the things he wanted to do to her, each word a dirty promise that made her ache with anticipation. He pulled her underwear aside, his fingers slipping between her folds to find her wet and willing.

Erika groaned as he entered her, the initial stretch a sharp contrast to the emptiness she'd felt for so long. They moved together, the rhythm of their bodies a testament to their mutual need. The world outside ceased to exist; there was only the feeling of Alex inside her, the sound of their mingled breaths, the taste of forbidden fruit on her tongue.

Their lovemaking was a tangle of limbs and whispers, of urgency and abandon. Erika felt herself spiraling towards the edge, each thrust of Alex's hips pushing her closer to the abyss. She clung to him, her nails digging into the fabric of his shirt as she shattered around him, her orgasm ripping through her like a wave crashing against the shore.

Alex, feeling her clinch tightly as she came followed close behind, his body shuddering as he found his release. They lay entwined on the couch, their breaths ragged, the scent of sex heavy in the air.

As they disentangled, reality began to seep back in. Erika's heart raced, not just from the exertion, but from the realization of what she'd done. She straightened her clothes, avoiding Alex's gaze, the weight of her actions pressing down on her.

"Thank you," she murmured, not sure what else to say. She was grateful, but also terrified of the path she'd just stepped onto.

Alex smiled at her, a smile that spoke of shared secrets and the promise of more to come. "Anytime, Erika," he said, the words a silent vow that their encounter was just the beginning.

Afterward, Erika felt a pang of guilt. But it was quickly over-shadowed by the thrill of the forbidden, the knowledge that she had stepped into a new chapter of her life—she knew that this was only the beginning. Her lunch breaks had taken on a whole new meaning, and she was already looking forward to the next one.

Erika checked her watch as she hurried through the hotel lobby. She was running five minutes late for her lunch meeting with Professor James Bennett, in town for an academic conference on comparative literature. Her heart raced, though not from the brisk walk.

The elevator climbed to the twelfth floor. When she knocked on room 1214, the door opened almost immediately.

"I was beginning to think you'd changed your mind." James stood before her, tall and lean with salt-and-pepper hair and wire-rimmed glasses that gave him an intellectual air that made her pulse quicken.

"Traffic." She stepped inside, her eyes taking in the spacious suite with its view of the city skyline.

"I ordered room service." He gestured to a small table by the window where a bottle of wine stood uncorked. "I hope you don't mind eating in. Privacy seemed... preferable."

Erika slipped off her coat. "I'm not really here for the food."

His eyes darkened behind those scholarly glasses. "No, I suppose you're not."

James closed the distance between them with two long strides. His kiss was different from Alex's—more measured, more deliberate. He tasted of mint and coffee, his hands moving with academic precision as they traced the curve of her waist.

"Tell me what you want," he murmured against her neck.

Erika found herself emboldened by the anonymity, by the knowledge that in three days, James would be back at his university hundreds of miles away. "I want you to make me forget everything except this moment."

He smiled, a slow curving of lips that promised he knew exactly how to deliver what she asked for. "I believe I can manage that."

His fingers worked at the buttons of her blouse with methodical patience. Unlike her frantic encounter with Alex, James took his time, each touch a deliberate exploration. He treated her body like a text to be studied, interpreted, understood.

"You're beautiful," he whispered, leading her toward the king-sized bed. "Absolutely exquisite."

Erika closed her eyes as his weight settled over her, his academic demeanor giving way to something primal and hungry.

James's kisses trailed down Erika's body, his tongue tracing a path to the soft, sensitive skin of her inner thighs. She quivered under his touch, her breath hitching as he hooked his fingers under the waistband of her panties and peeled them away.

Erika's heart pounded in her chest, a staccato rhythm that matched the throbbing between her legs. She reached for him, her hands fumbling with his belt, eager to free him from his trousers. His member sprang forth, hard and ready, and she wrapped her fingers around its girth, feeling a thrill at the soft gasp that escaped his lips.

With a gentle nudge, James guided her onto her side, positioning himself so that they faced each other's most intimate parts. Erika's pulse quickened as she took in the sight of him, so close to her mouth, and she licked her lips in anticipation.

Their bodies instinctively finding the rhythm that would bring them both to the edge. Erika took him into her mouth, her tongue swirling around the head of his cock, tasting the salty essence of him. James groaned, the vibration traveling through her as he reciprocated, his tongue delving into her folds, finding her clitoris and teasing it mercilessly.

Erika moaned around James, the sound muffled by his flesh in her mouth. She sucked harder, her hand cupping his balls, feeling them tighten in response to her ministrations. James's fingers dug into her hips, his own moans of pleasure mingling with hers as they lost themselves in the act.

The world outside the hotel room faded into nothingness, leaving only the scent, the taste, and the sensation of their bodies intertwined. Erika's climax built within her, a tide of pleasure that threatened to sweep her away. She fought to maintain her focus on James, wanting—needing—to bring him to release as her own body teetered on the brink.

James's movements became more frenzied, his tongue working with feverish intensity as he sensed her nearing the point of no return. Erika's orgasm hit her like a wave, her body convulsing as she cried out around his cock. James followed her over the edge, his hot release spilling into her mouth as he shuddered against her.

They lay there for a moment, their bodies slick with sweat, their breaths ragged and uneven. Slowly, they untangled themselves, coming to rest side by side, their limbs still entwined. James's hand found hers, their fingers interlacing in the afterglow of their shared passion.

The room was silent except for their breathing, the city skyline a distant backdrop to the intimacy they had just shared. Erika turned her head to look at James, his glasses askew and his hair tousled, a satisfied smile playing on his lips. She returned the smile, feeling a connection that was both unexpected and deeply, deeply satisfying.

Erika's heart thrummed with a desperate need that had been too long ignored. She rolled onto her hands and knees, the cool sheets of the hotel bed bunching under her palms. Glancing over her shoulder, she met James's gaze, her eyes smoldering with unspoken desires.

"James," she said, her voice firm yet laced with a vulnerability that surprised her. "I want you to fuck me. Can you get hard again if I suck you some more?"

James's breath caught, and for a moment, Erika saw a flicker of uncertainty cross his face. "I think so," he replied, his voice slightly hoarse and hesitant.

With a determined nod, Erika moved her head once again to where James's cock lay against his thigh, still glistening from their earlier tryst. She began gently teasing it with her fingertips, stroking the soft skin until it began to respond, growing and hardening beneath her touch.

Her mouth followed her hands, her tongue darting out to taste him, to coax him back to full attention. She took him into her mouth, her lips closing around his shaft, her head bobbing in a slow, deliberate rhythm.

James's fingers tangled in her hair, guiding her without forcing her, his hips subtly rocking in time with her movements. Within minutes, his cock was hard once again, rigid and throbbing with renewed desire.

Erika rose and positioned herself on all fours, her back arched, her ass high in the air, fully exposed to James' hungry glare. She looked back at James, her gaze unwavering, a silent dare hanging between them.

"Take me, James," she commanded, her voice steady despite the pounding of her heart. "Fuck me senseless. I need this. I need more!"

James's eyes darkened, all traces of hesitation gone, replaced by a fierce hunger. He moved behind her, his hands gripping her hips, his fingers digging into her flesh.

With one swift motion, he plunged into her, filling her completely. Erika gasped, her body stretching to accommodate him, a sensation that bordered on pain but was quickly replaced by a deep, satisfying fullness.

James set a punishing pace, each thrust eliciting a cry from Erika's lips, each withdrawal leaving her momentarily empty, aching to be filled once more. She pushed back against him, meeting each of his thrusts with an eagerness that matched his own.

The room was filled with the sounds of their coupling—flesh slapping against flesh, their shared moans of pleasure, the wet suction of their bodies joining and parting.

Erika's orgasm built within her, a slow burn that rapidly grew into an uncontrollable inferno. She felt herself teetering on the edge, her muscles clenching around James's cock as she neared the precipice.

"Harder, James," she begged, her voice ragged with need. "Make me come. Fucking, make me come!"

James obliged, his hips pistoning against her with increased fervor, his climax rapidly approaching, his cock pulsing spilling his seed once more deep within her as he rode out his orgasm, his fingers bruising as he held her tight, spilling himself into her with a final, shuddering thrust.

Erika could feel the warm gush fill her as her body shook with the force of her own release, a wave of pleasure crashing over her, her cries of ecstasy echoing off the hotel walls.

They collapsed onto the bed, their bodies slick with sweat and tangled in the sheets, their breaths coming in ragged gasps. James pulled Erika close, her back to his chest, his cock still nestled inside her.

For a moment, they lay there in silence, the only sound their mingled breaths as they gradually returned to normal. Erika could feel James's heart beating against her back, a steady rhythm that matched her own.

As their bodies cooled and their breathing evened out, Erika felt a sense of peace wash over her. In James's arms, she had found a temporary respite from the emptiness that had consumed her for so long.

But as the euphoria of their coupling began to fade, the reality of her situation crept back in. She was a married woman, a mother, caught in a web of desire and deception that she had spun with her own hands.

Erika closed her eyes, pushing the thought away. For now, she would allow herself this indulgence, this moment of escape. Tomorrow could wait.

In this hotel room, with this stranger, she wasn't a neglected wife or an invisible mother. She was desired, wanted, seen.

Erika sipped her coffee and scrolled through her dating app messages with methodical precision. The familiar rush of adrenaline coursed through her veins as she filtered through potential candidates. What had started as a quest for simple attention had evolved into something more complex, more demanding.

Her finger paused over a message from a man named Kyle. His profile photo showed only his torso—muscular, with a tattoo snaking up his side. Unlike her previous encounters, Kyle had been direct about his preferences. Things she'd never considered. Acts that made her blush when she first read his suggestions.

"I could never," she had initially thought. Yet here she was, three days later, composing a reply that made her heart race.

I'm interested. Friday, 2 PM. Send hotel and room number.

She added one more line before hitting send:

Bring what you mentioned. I want to try everything.

Erika set her phone down, her hand trembling slightly. This was different from her previous encounters—calculated affairs with clear boundaries. Kyle represented something altogether new: a deliberate step into the unknown, into desires she'd never acknowledged even to herself.

In her diary that night, she wrote:

Dear diary,

I've made a list of things I want to experience. Things I never dared ask Michael for. Things I never even knew I wanted until now. With each new encounter, I find myself craving more intensity, more risk. The boundaries I set at the beginning seem arbitrary now. What's one more step across a line I've already crossed?

Kyle suggested things that would have horrified me six months ago. Now I'm counting the hours until Friday. What does that say about me?

She paused, pen hovering over the page, before continuing:

I told him to bring restraints. I told him I want to feel helpless, to surrender control completely. To be used in ways I've only read about. The thought terrifies and thrills me in equal measure.

Who am I becoming?

Erika closed her diary and locked it in her desk drawer. She checked her secret credit card statement online, calculating how much room remained for hotel charges before Michael might notice discrepancies in their finances. She was getting careless with her alibis, rushing through explanations about her whereabouts.

The risk only heightened her anticipation for Friday.

CHAPTER SIXTEEN

Close Call

F riday arrived with thunderclouds gathering on the hori-
zon. Erika walked into the downtown hotel thirty minutes early, her nerves humming beneath her carefully applied
makeup. She'd told Michael she was meeting a potential new
bookkeeping client who needed extensive help organizing their
finances—another lie that rolled off her tongue with disturbing
ease.

The elevator ascended smoothly to the seventh floor. Erika checked her appearance in the mirrored wall, adjusting her
blouse and tucking a strand of hair behind her ear. The doors
opened, and she stepped out, consulting her phone for the room
number Kyle had sent.

"Erika? Is that you?"

The voice froze her mid-step. She knew that chirpy, perfectionist tone anywhere. Slowly, Erika turned to face the last person she wanted to encounter.

"Jessica. Hi." Her mouth went dry as she faced the PTA president—the woman who organized every school fundraiser with military precision and judged other mothers' contributions with thinly veiled contempt.

Jessica Whitman stood in the hallway clutching a portfolio case, her blonde hair pulled into its signature tight bun. "What a surprise! Are you staying here?"

"No, I—" Erika's mind raced. "Just meeting a client. Bookkeeping consultation."

Jessica's eyes narrowed slightly. "How funny. I'm here for the regional PTA leadership conference. We're using the conference rooms downstairs." She glanced at Erika's outfit—the silk blouse and pencil skirt that had seemed professional enough but now felt like an obvious costume. "Didn't realize bookkeepers made house calls to hotels."

"Some clients prefer neutral meeting spaces." The lie sounded hollow even to Erika's ears.

Jessica checked her watch. "Well, I should get back downstairs. We're discussing fundraising strategies for next semester." She paused, her gaze drifting to Erika's left hand where her wedding ring was conspicuously absent. "Will we see you at the committee meeting on Tuesday? We really need more parent volunteers."

"I'll try," Erika managed, heart pounding. "Depends on my schedule."

Jessica nodded, her smile not reaching her eyes. "Of course. Well, good luck with your... client."

Erika pressed her back against the wall as Jessica disappeared into the elevator. Her heart hammered against her ribs, each beat a warning she chose to ignore. She should leave. She should text Kyle and cancel. She should go home to her family.

Instead, she found herself walking faster toward room 712, her pulse racing with something that wasn't entirely fear.

The near-discovery should have terrified her. Instead, adrenaline coursed through her veins, making her fingertips tingle. She knocked on Kyle's door with more confidence than she'd felt minutes earlier.

"You look flushed," Kyle said when he opened the door. Tall and broad-shouldered with dark eyes that missed nothing, he stepped aside to let her in.

"I just ran into someone I know in the hallway." Erika moved past him, catching his cologne—something expensive and subtle. "A PTA mom from my kids' school."

Kyle's eyebrows rose. "Problem?"

Erika surprised herself by laughing. "I made up some excuse about meeting a client. She didn't believe me."

"And that's... funny?"

She turned to face him, dropping her purse on the desk chair. "It should be terrifying. I should be running out of here."

Kyle studied her, keeping a careful distance. "But you're not."

"No." Erika moved toward him, close enough to feel the heat radiating from his body. "I'm not."

The realization crashed over her—the near-miss with Jessica had left her not panicked but electrified. The danger of discovery, the secret thrill of almost being caught—it heightened everything. Made the forbidden more enticing.

"Maybe I'm more reckless than I thought," she whispered, reaching for his belt.

Kyle caught her wrist, his grip firm. "Tell me what you want."

"I want to forget who I'm supposed to be." She met his gaze without flinching. "And I want to not care who might find out."

Later, as Kyle slept beside her, Erika stared at the ceiling. She should be rushing home, covering her tracks. Instead, she savored the lingering danger. She pictured Jessica's suspicious face, Michael's trusting one, and felt a twisted thrill at balancing between her worlds.

The fear of discovery wasn't driving her away from these encounters—it was becoming part of the attraction.

CHAPTER SEVENTEEN

The App Collection

E rika sat cross-legged on her bed, phone in hand, the house empty on a Tuesday afternoon. Three dating apps resided in a folder labeled "Work Tools" on her second screen—hidden in plain sight should Michael ever glance at her phone.

She swiped through profiles on the first app, where she was "Erika, 35, separated marketing consultant" with photos that showed her body but obscured her face with strategic angles and lighting. This was her "adventurous" profile, where she matched with men looking for no-strings encounters.

A notification pinged from her second app. She switched over, where "Erin, 38, widow and entrepreneur" existed in carefully constructed detail. Here, her photos were softer, more demure—a fabricated backstory about losing her husband three years ago and finally feeling ready to connect again. This persona attracted a different type: protective men who wanted to "take care" of her, who messaged with respectful patience and treated her like fine china.

The third app was newest, and the most dangerous. "Kate, 32, open marriage" featured her most revealing photos and brazen bio. This version of herself matched with couples and men in similar arrangements, people who understood discretion because they needed it too.

Erika had created spreadsheets to keep track of her lies—the ages of fictional children, made-up career details, which men knew what information. She'd developed systems for scheduling, ensuring encounters never overlapped with family obligations. She maintained separate email accounts for each persona and had even purchased yet another phone for the riskier connections.

What had started as a single secret profile had evolved into a complex operation. Each persona allowed her to explore different aspects of herself—the vixen, the vulnerable, the voyeur—versions of Erika that couldn't exist within the confines of her marriage.

She switched between apps methodically, responding to messages in the appropriate voice for each character she'd created. The businessman who thought she was a widow. The professor who believed she was separated. The couple who thought she had an understanding with her husband.

"Mom? You home?" Zach's voice called from downstairs.

Erika quickly closed the apps and slipped her phone under her pillow. "Up here, honey! Just sorting some laundry!"

The seamless transition between her worlds frightened her less each time she made it.

"So this is what, the third guy this week?" Natalie stirred her margarita, eyebrow raised. They sat in a corner booth at Castillo's, their usual spot for Thursday happy hours.

Erika shrugged, defensive. "It's just lunch breaks. I'm not taking time away from the kids."

"That's not what I'm worried about." Natalie leaned forward, lowering her voice. "I'm all for sexual liberation, but this is starting to feel... compulsive."

"Says the woman who encouraged me to download the apps in the first place."

"For occasional fun, not a part-time job." Natalie's eyes softened. "You've got spreadsheets, Erika. Multiple phones. You're cataloging men like they're rare books."

Erika took a long sip of her drink, avoiding Natalie's gaze. The truth stung—she'd spent the morning color-coding her encounter spreadsheet, adding detailed notes about a lawyer she'd met yesterday in a downtown hotel.

"I'm making up for lost time."

"Are you? Because it looks more like you're running from something." Natalie reached across the table, squeezing Erika's hand. "Last month, you told me about that guy from Cincinnati—the one with the sailboat. You couldn't remember his real name mid-story because you'd saved him in your phone as 'Blue Shirt Hotel Bar.'"

Heat crept up Erika's neck. "That was a slip-up."

"It was a warning sign. These aren't even people to you anymore—they're experiences to collect."

Erika pulled her hand away. "You don't understand. When I'm with them, I'm seen. I matter."

"For an hour in a hotel room."

"That's better than nothing."

Natalie sighed, swirling the salt rim of her glass. "Remember when you first told me about the trainer? You were alive with guilt and excitement. Now you talk about these encounters like you're reading a shopping list."

"What exactly are you saying?"

"I'm saying I'm worried. This isn't just about sex anymore. It's about filling something that keeps getting bigger." Natalie hesitated. "Maybe it's time to talk to someone. A professional."

CHAPTER EIGHTEEN

The Bar Pickup

E rika left the restaurant fuming. Who was Natalie to judge? Her phone buzzed with a notification from her primary dating app—another match, another possibility. She silenced it, shoving the device deep into her purse.

The evening air felt heavy with impending rain as she cut through Riverside Park, taking the shortcut to her car. Halfway across the empty park, fat droplets began falling. She quickened her pace, heels clicking against the pavement.

"Need this?"

A man appeared beside her, extending an umbrella. Tall, broad-shouldered, with salt-and-pepper hair and a tailored suit that suggested money. Not her usual type—she preferred younger, hungrier men who wouldn't ask questions.

"Thanks." She stepped under the umbrellas' shelter, their shoulders brushing. "Wasn't expecting the downpour."

"Weather app said clear skies. Shows what they know." His voice carried a slight accent—European, refined.

They walked in silence for a moment, their footsteps synchronizing naturally.

"Bad day?" he asked.

"That obvious?"

"Your shoulders are practically touching your ears." He smiled—warm, disarming. "I'm David."

"Erika."

No last names. Perfect.

The rain intensified, drumming against the umbrellas' canopy. They reached the edge of the park, where the path forked.

"My car's that way," she pointed.

"Mine too."

Lightning flashed, followed by a thunderclap that made her jump. His hand steadied her elbow, lingering longer than necessary. She felt the familiar flutter—possibility, danger.

"There's a café around the corner," he said. "Wait out the storm?"

No profile to scrutinize. No messages exchanged. No careful vetting. Just a stranger with kind eyes and a wedding band that matched her own.

"Lead the way."

They ducked into a dimly lit wine bar instead, sliding into a booth at the back. One glass became two. She learned he was a visiting professor from London, giving a series of lectures at the university. She told him she worked in finance—her standard lie.

When his knee pressed against hers under the table, she didn't move away. When his fingers brushed hers while reaching for the wine list, she felt electricity she hadn't experienced in weeks.

No spreadsheet entry. No planning. Just pure, dangerous impulse.

The storm intensified, rattling the windows of the wine bar. David ordered a second round, his fingers lingering on the stem of his glass.

"So you're not going to tell me what had you walking through a park alone at night with that expression?" He leaned closer, cologne subtle but expensive.

"Just a disagreement with a friend." Erika sipped her wine. "She thinks I'm... making poor choices lately."

"And are you?"

"Probably." She met his eyes directly. "But they feel good."

The waiter appeared with their drinks. David raised his glass. "To poor choices that feel good."

The wine tasted better than it should, or maybe it was the company. She found herself studying him—the way his cuffs revealed expensive links, how his eyes crinkled when he laughed. No dating profile could have captured the magnetic pull she felt.

"Your lectures," she asked, "what are they about?"

"Behavioral economics. Decision-making under risk." His thumb traced circles on the back of her hand. "How people choose short-term rewards over long-term stability."

"Sounds relevant to my current situation."

"Does it?" His smile was knowing, dangerous.

Erika checked her watch. The kids would be in bed by now. Michael had texted earlier—working late again. No one expecting her home soon.

"I should go." She didn't move.

"Should you?" His knee pressed more firmly against hers.

The rain pounded against the windows. Lightning flashed, illuminating his face—handsome, confident, temporary.

"My hotel is three blocks away." He didn't phrase it as a question.

Erika drained her glass, decision already made. "Lead the way."

He paid the bill without checking the amount, helped her into her coat with practiced ease. Outside, the rain had slowed to a drizzle. He held the umbrella over them both, his hand settling naturally at the small of her back.

No messages exchanged beforehand. No safety protocols. No alias carefully constructed. Just pure impulse—the most dangerous encounter yet.

They walked in silence, her pulse thundering in her ears. At the hotel entrance, he paused, giving her one last chance to walk away.

She stepped through the door first.

Dear diary,

I've lost track of the days, the faces, the names. They blend and blur in my memory, each encounter a forgotten chapter until tonight. Tonight, I write with trembling hands, the echoes of pleasure still reverberating through me.

David was different from the start. There was no premeditated seduction, no carefully selected outfits or coy glances across a crowded room. He was there, an umbrella in the storm, a stranger with eyes that promised secrets and warmth.

We spoke of nothing and everything, our words a mere prelude to the symphony of sounds we would soon create. The wine was a poor excuse for liquid courage, but it was the rain—the wild, unpredictable rain—that whispered of desire unchained.

His hotel room was an extension of him—understated elegance, with a view that overlooked the city's twinkling lights. I remember standing there, the door barely closed behind us, and feeling as though I was suspended in time, caught between the woman I was and the woman I've become.

David approached me, his movements deliberate, his eyes never leaving mine. When he kissed me, it was with a tenderness that belied the urgency of our need. His hands, skilled and confident, explored my body as if he had all the time in the world, yet every touch conveyed a sense of exquisite impatience.

We undressed each other slowly, savoring the reveal of each new inch of skin. He laid me down on the bed, his body covering mine, the weight of him both a comfort and a thrill. The sex was a dance—sometimes frenzied, sometimes slow, always in perfect rhythm.

I found myself saying yes to things I never imagined, my inhibitions stripped away as easily as my clothes. There was a freedom in the anonymity, a heightened sense of pleasure in the risk we were taking. Every moan, every gasp, every shudder was magnified because we were strangers, because this was fleeting, because tomorrow didn't exist in that room.

The intensity of our coupling left me breathless, my body humming with a satisfaction so deep it bordered on pain. And when we were spent, when the fervor had subsided and our breathing had slowed, there was a quiet understanding between us—no pretense, no promises, just the shared knowledge of a connection that was as real as it was ephemeral.

I left his room in the early hours of the morning, the city still asleep. The cool air of the hallway hit my bare skin, a stark contrast to the warmth I was leaving behind. As I slipped my shoes on in the elevator, I caught a glimpse of myself in the mirror—flushed, tousled, alive.

It was then that I understood. The immediacy, the risk, the absence of pretense—all of it amplified my pleasure in ways I hadn't anticipated. There is a potent allure to these anonymous encounters, a dangerous dance with desire and the unknown. It's as if I've unlocked a part of myself that I never knew existed, and now, I'm not sure I can—or even want to—put it back in its cage.

For now, I am sated, but the hunger that drives me is insatiable. It whispers promises of future rendezvous, of secret trysts yet to come. I am walking a precarious tightrope, balancing precariously between the life I know and the desires that threaten to consume me.

But for tonight, I am content to bask in the afterglow, to relive the encounter through the ink that flows from my pen. David, with his umbrella and his easy smile, will be a memory that lingers, a chapter in my life that I will not soon forget.

I close my diary, the pages filled with the truth of my transgressions. Sleep comes quickly, a peaceful interlude before the dawn brings with it the sobering reality of my choices. But for these few, precious hours, I am exactly where I want to be—embraced by shadows and the sweet, intoxicating taste of freedom.

CHAPTER NINETEEN

Two in One Day

The hotel's breakfast buffet hummed with business travelers when I arrived. I'd chosen a place twenty miles from home, where the chances of running into someone I knew hovered near zero. My watch read 7:45 AM – fifteen minutes early for my morning rendezvous with Daniel, a pharmaceutical rep passing through town.

Morning meetings carried less suspicion. I could be "having coffee with a client" or "dropping documents at the accountant's office." The daylight made everything seem less sordid somehow, though the intention remained unchanged.

I selected a corner table with my back to the wall, ordered coffee, and pulled out my phone. Three texts from Michael asking where the permission slip for Zach's field trip was. I answered quickly, then switched to my other messaging app.

"Just got here. Corner table, blue blouse," I typed to Daniel.

The coffee arrived, and I wrapped my hands around the warm mug, steadying nerves that should have calmed by now. This was my fifth morning meet-up, yet the initial flutter of anticipation never diminished.

I spotted him before he saw me – tall with dark hair, scanning the room with confident ease. Our eyes met, and his smile confirmed I was his target. The wedding band on his left hand caught the light as he approached.

"Erika?" His voice carried just enough to reach me, not enough to turn heads.

"Daniel. Nice to finally meet you."

He sat down, ordered coffee, and we fell into the practiced small talk of strangers with limited time and specific intentions. His knee brushed mine under the table – an accident at first, then deliberate as our conversation shifted to why we were really here.

"My room's just upstairs," he said, glancing at his watch. "I have a late checkout."

The directness was refreshing. No pretense of wanting more than what this was.

"I have an hour," I replied, gathering my purse.

We walked separately to the elevator, maintaining the polite distance of business acquaintances in the lobby. Only when the doors closed did his hand find the small of my back and slowly move down to feel the firmness of my ass, his cologne enveloping me as the numbers climbed toward his floor.

The digital clock on my dashboard read 9:17 PM. I'd told Michael I was meeting Natalie for drinks after a long day with difficult clients. Another lie that slipped from my lips with disturbing ease.

I parked three blocks from The Velvet Room, a dimly lit cocktail bar downtown where no soccer moms or PTA members would venture. My reflection in the rearview mirror showed a woman I barely recognized – hair loosely curled, eyes darkened with smoky shadow, lips painted a shade I'd never wear to carpool.

The morning's hotel encounter with Daniel had been efficient, satisfying in the mechanical way these meetings often were. But as I'd driven home, a hollow feeling expanded in my chest. The spreadsheet entry would be unremarkable – another 6/10 experience with nothing distinctive to note.

I needed something unplanned. Something real.

The bar's interior glowed amber, half-full with Tuesday night patrons – mostly professionals unwinding after work. I claimed a stool at the counter, ordered a gin martini, and waited. Not for anyone specific. Just waited.

"This seat taken?"

I turned to find a man about my age, maybe younger, with dark eyes and a five o'clock shadow that looked deliberate rather than neglected.

"It's all yours." I gestured to the empty stool.

"I'm Ryan." No wedding ring, I noticed. A rarity in my recent catalog of men.

"Erika." My real name slipped out before I could catch it.

"Drinking alone on a Tuesday. That's either a very good day or a very bad one."

I swirled the olive in my martini. "Neither. Just... escaping."

"Aren't we all?" He raised his whiskey glass in a small toast.

Two drinks later, we'd moved to a booth in the corner. His hand rested on my knee, thumb tracing small circles that sent electricity up my thigh.

Beneath the table, my hand ventured further, guided by the magnetic pull of our connection. The low hum of bar chatter and clinking glassware faded into the background as my fingers traced the length of him through the fabric of his trousers.

Ryan's breath caught subtly, a small hitch that only I could detect in the semi-privacy of our booth. His eyes, dark as the whiskey he'd been drinking, locked onto mine with an intensity that belied the casual conversation we'd been maintaining.

"Erika," he murmured, my name a question and a plea on his lips.

I didn't respond with words. Instead, I let my touch speak for me, feeling the hardening evidence of his desire grow beneath my palm. The sensation of him, thick and insistent, sent a jolt of heady power through me, a reminder that I was still desirable, still capable of igniting such a raw, carnal response.

His hand, which had been resting on my knee, now gripped it firmly, his fingers exerting a gentle pressure that seemed to say, "Yes, this is real." Encouraged, I grew bolder, my movements more deliberate, tracing the contours of his arousal with increasing confidence.

The air between us was charged, the space in the booth suddenly too small, too confined for the fire that was building. I could feel the heat of his thigh against mine, the warmth of his body so close to mine, yet not close enough.

Ryan's other hand reached across the table, taking my free hand in his, his thumb caressing my palm. It was an anchor in the tempest of our rising desire, a point of connection that was both tender and tantalizingly erotic.

I knew we couldn't stay here, in this bar, much longer. The pretense of casual conversation was rapidly unraveling, the undercurrent of our true intentions becoming harder to conceal. I gave him a squeeze, a silent promise of what was to come, and his response was a low, almost imperceptible groan of longing.

"Let's get out of here," I whispered, my voice barely audible over the din of the bar.

Ryan nodded, his gaze never leaving mine. We stood up, our bodies brushing against each other as we navigated the tight space of the booth. The fleeting contact was electric, a prelude to the storm we were about to unleash.

As we made our way to the exit, our strides matched, our hands still entwined, I felt alive in a way I hadn't in years. This was uncharted territory, a leap into the unknown with a man whose last name I didn't even know. And yet, it felt right. It felt necessary.

Outside, the cool night air enveloped us, a stark contrast to the heat that had been building within the walls of The Velvet Room. Ryan hailed a cab, and as we slid into the backseat, our bodies pressed together in the intimate confines of the vehicle, I knew that this night would be one I'd revisit in my diary, a chapter in my life that was raw, unpredictable, and undeniably exhilarating.

We hadn't discussed intentions or boundaries. No messages exchanged beforehand outlining expectations. Just pure chemistry and unspoken understanding.

"My place is close," he said, his breath warm against my ear.

I nodded, "Close sounds perfect."

Dear diary,

It's been a whirlwind since my last entry. The encounter with Ryan at the bar feels like it happened in another life, yet the taste of his whiskey-laced kiss is still on my lips. That night, the raw hunger in his eyes ignited something within me that I can't seem to extinguish. Ryan was my second encounter that day.

When we made it to his place, our clothes became a forgotten trail leading to his bedroom. The urgency in his hands as they explored my body was both thrilling and affirming. Every touch, every kiss, felt like a discovery of something I'd long forgotten—my own sensuality.

Lying in his bed, the moonlight spilling across our entwined bodies, I reveled in the novelty of his skin against mine. The solid weight of him pressing me into the mattress, the rasp of his stubble against my neck, the salty taste of his skin—it was a symphony of sensation, overwhelming and intoxicating.

Ryan's hands roamed freely, his touch a mixture of reverence and raw need. He worshiped my body with an intensity that left me breathless, worshiped it as if it were a temple that he'd been seeking his entire life. And in that moment, I allowed myself to believe it.

The sex was frenzied, almost desperate. We were two strangers clinging to each other in the dark, seeking solace in the physical connection that we both craved. With each thrust, I felt the walls I'd built around myself beginning to crack. I was consumed by the sheer carnality of it all.

Afterwards, as we lay spent in the tangle of his sheets, the silence was not uncomfortable, but acknowledging. We shared something powerful, something that transcended the casual encounters I'd become accustomed to. It was genuine, and that terrified me.

Despite the intensity of our connection, or perhaps because of it, I find myself grappling with a sense of emptiness once again. The high of our encounter is fading, replaced by a gnawing hunger for more. I'm chasing a feeling that seems to slip through my fingers the moment I grasp it.

I've become acutely aware of the void in my marriage, a void that Ryan, for a fleeting moment, filled. But it's not enough. The frequency of my trysts has increased, a never-ending quest to recapture that initial rush of excitement and desire. I'm caught in a cycle of seeking validation through the eyes of strangers, the thrill of their touch a fleeting balm for a wound that refuses to heal.

I tell myself that it's just physical, that these encounters mean nothing, but the truth is more complicated. Each man I bring to my bed is another step away from the woman I used to be, the one who believed in love and fidelity. Yet, the thought of stopping, of returning to my old life, is unbearable.

I'm not sure where this path will lead, but I can't deny the pull it has on me. The taste of freedom, the intoxicating allure of the unknown—they've become my siren song, luring me further into the depths of my own desires.

For now, I continue to document each encounter, each fleeting connection, in these pages. Perhaps one day, I'll find what I'm looking for. But until then, I'll keep searching in the arms of strangers, hoping to find a piece of myself in their embrace.

CHAPTER TWENTY

The Threesome Proposition

The notification popped up on my phone while I was stirring pasta for the kids' dinner. A new message on the dating app I'd labeled "Echo" on my home screen—the one where my profile showed only my silhouette against a sunset.

"We've been admiring your profile," the message read. "Both of us."

I nearly dropped the wooden spoon. My thumb hovered over the message. Both? I clicked through to their profile—"Mark&Jen35"—and found myself staring at a photograph of an attractive couple. He was tall with brown hair and a confident smile. She was petite with chestnut waves and bright eyes that crinkled at the corners.

"Mom, is the pasta done?" Lily called from the living room.

"Almost," I answered, my voice steadier than I felt.

After dinner and homework checks, I retreated to my bathroom, locked the door, and opened the message again.

"We're both experienced and respectful," they'd written. "Something about your profile intrigued us. We'd love to meet for drinks, no pressure, and see if there's chemistry. We have a hotel downtown next Saturday."

My heart hammered against my ribs. A couple. A threesome. This was uncharted territory, even for the new Erika. In all my spreadsheets and ratings, I'd never encountered this possibility, but it was on my secret bucket list after all.

I studied their photos again. They looked normal—successful, attractive, the kind of couple you'd see at a neighborhood barbecue. Not predators or creeps. Just people seeking connection, like me.

The cursor blinked on my phone's screen, mocking me with its relentless tick. My initial thought was to delete the message, block the profile, and pretend this hadn't happened. It was too far, too risky.

But as I lay in bed that night, Michael's soft snores filling the silence, I couldn't shake the image of Mark and Jen from my mind. The way his arm was draped casually over her shoulder, the warmth in their eyes as they looked at the camera—a stark contrast to the cool detachment I'd grown accustomed to at home.

I imagined myself with them, the sensation of unfamiliar hands on my skin, the thrill of being the center of such intense, shared attention. It was a fantasy so far removed from my reality that it seemed to belong to someone else entirely. Yet, the longer I let the scenario unfold in my head, the more the nervous flutter in my stomach gave way to a simmering heat.

The next morning, while the kids were at school and Michael was buried in his work, I found myself replying to Mark and Jen's message. "I'm intrigued," I typed, my fingers trembling. "Let's meet for drinks."

Their response came quickly, eagerly. "We can't wait to meet you. Next Saturday, 8 PM, The Rendezvous Lounge. We'll be the couple smiling at the bar."

The week crawled by, each day a blend of mundane routines and electric anticipation. I found myself staring into space, lost in thoughts of what might happen. The scenarios I played out in my head were wildly erotic, a kaleidoscope of sensations that left me simultaneously terrified and exhilarated.

I told Natalie about the upcoming meet, watching her eyes widen in surprise before a slow, knowing smile spread across her face. "You're really going for it, aren't you?" she said, a mix of admiration and concern lacing her voice.

"I think I need to," I confessed. "I need to know what it's like, just once."

Saturday finally arrived. I stood in front of the mirror, smoothing down the black dress I'd chosen—elegant yet undeniably sexy. The woman who looked back at me was a stranger, her eyes alight with a fire that had been smoldering for too long.

Michael barely looked up from his laptop as I told him I was meeting Natalie for a late drink. "Don't wait up," I said, the words tasting like freedom on my tongue.

The Rendezvous Lounge was dimly lit and buzzing with the low hum of conversation. As I scanned the room, a couple at the bar caught my eye. Mark and Jen. They were even more attractive in person, their smiles genuine and inviting.

My heart raced as I approached, the reality of what I was about to do settling over me. I took a deep breath and returned their smiles with one of my own.

"Hi," I said, stepping into their world for the night. "I'm Erika."

The hostess led us to a secluded booth, a plush semicircle of dark leather that promised privacy. I slid in first, my back to the wall, and they followed, Mark on my left, Jen on my right, a living embodiment of the balance I was seeking.

The waitress came by, and we ordered a round of drinks, the clink of glassware and murmur of the lounge providing a sooth-ing backdrop to the thrum of my pulse. As the conversation began, it was stilted, peppered with safe topics like work and hobbies, the weather, and the latest box office hit.

But as the alcohol warmed our blood, the exchanges grew bolder, more intimate. Mark's eyes, a vivid shade of blue, held mine as he spoke of his fantasies. "I've always been drawn to the idea of dual beauty, two women who complement each other in every way," he confessed, his voice a low rumble. "The sensuality, the energy, it's... it's art in motion."

Jen's hand found mine under the table, her fingers intertwining with my own. "And I've always wondered what it would be like to explore that side of myself, to be with another woman," she admitted, her voice barely above a whisper. "To feel that connection and to share it with someone I love."

They spoke of their previous encounters, the nervous excitement, the tender exploration, the exhilarating release of inhibitions. Their words painted a vivid picture of passion and trust, a dance of desire that left me both envious and eager to join in.

"We've found something incredible," Mark said, his hand now resting on Jen's thigh, a silent testament to their bond. "It's deepened our relationship in ways we never imagined."

Jen nodded, her eyes shining. "It's not just about the physical. It's about the emotional openness, the vulnerability we share. It's brought us closer."

Their honesty was a balm to my long-suppressed desires. Here, in this dimly lit booth, I felt seen and understood in a way I hadn't in years. It was as if they'd peered into the depths of my soul and saw the same yearning that I'd kept hidden, even from myself.

As the night wore on, the air around us grew thick with anticipation. The space between us seemed to hum with unspoken promises, our bodies subtly leaning in, drawn together by a magnetic force we no longer wished to resist.

Mark's hand moved from Jen's thigh to mine, his thumb stroking the soft fabric of my dress, tracing small, tantalizing circles. Jen's gaze met mine, a silent question lingering in her eyes.

I nodded, a silent answer that needed no words. This was really happening. My heart raced with the thrill of it all, the newness, the naughtiness, the sense of adventure that had been absent for far too long in my life.

"Let's get out of here," Mark suggested, the timbre of his voice an intoxicating blend of command and suggestion.

We stood as one, our movements fluid, in sync, as if we'd done this a hundred times before. The short walk to the elevator was a blur of heated glances and stifled smiles, each of us aware that we were on the precipice of something extraordinary.

As the doors closed behind us, sealing us into our own private world, I realized that this wasn't just about seeking pleasure. It was about reclaiming a part of myself that I'd let wither in the shadow of neglect. Tonight, I was stepping back into the light.

The elevator doors whispered open, revealing the luxurious suite Mark and Jen had booked for the night. The space was a symphony of indulgence, from the plush carpet that sank underfoot to the floor-to-ceiling windows that offered a panoramic view of the city's twinkling lights.

As we stepped inside, the energy shifted, becoming more charged, more potent. Mark and Jen positioned themselves on either side of me, a silent pact sealed between us. I could feel the heat radiating from their bodies, could smell the faint trace of their colognes mingling in the air—his a rich, woodsy scent, hers a delicate floral.

Jen turned to me, her eyes dark with desire. "I think you want to kiss him," she said, her voice a sultry whisper that seemed to echo the pounding of my heart.

Without a moment's hesitation, I turned to Mark. Our eyes locked, and in that instant, the world seemed to shrink down to just the two of us. I leaned in, closing the space between us, and our lips met in a kiss that was both a question and an answer. His mouth was warm, his kiss confident and commanding, pulling me deeper into the whirlpool of this new experience.

As our kiss deepened, a hand—Jen's—grazed the small of my back, a gentle reminder that I was not alone with Mark. The realization sent a jolt of electricity through me, a thrilling shock that amplified the sensations coursing through my body.

When Mark finally broke the kiss, he looked at me with a mixture of hunger and admiration. "Have you ever kissed a girl, Erika?" he asked, his voice low and husky.

I felt my cheeks flush with a combination of arousal and embarrassment. "No," I admitted, my voice barely louder than a whisper.

"Would you like to?" His question hung in the air, a tantalizing invitation.

I hesitated for a fraction of a second before nodding, my eyes meeting Jen's. There was no judgment in her gaze, only a genuine curiosity and a shared desire for exploration.

Jen stepped closer, eliminating the last sliver of space that separated us. She reached up, her fingers lightly tracing the contours of my face before guiding my lips to hers. The kiss was soft at first, tentative, as if we were both discovering a new landscape. But as our mouths moved together, the initial shyness gave way to an urgency that was both surprising and exhilarating.

Our kiss was a dance of tongues and teeth, a delicious tangle of lips that left me breathless and yearning for more. Jen's hands roamed over my body, her touch igniting a fiery trail of goosebumps in their wake.

When we finally pulled apart, the three of us stood there, a triangle of shared desire, each of us aware that we had crossed a threshold into uncharted territory. The air was thick with anticipation, each breath a testament to the heat that had been kindled in this room.

Mark's hand found mine, and Jen's clasped the other, their grips a silent promise of the pleasures that lay ahead.

The soft glow of the bedside lamp cast a warm light over the room, throwing the opulence of the suite into sharp relief. Mark and Jen led me to the bed, their hands a gentle guide.

Once there, they stood before me, a united front, their eyes drinking in the sight of me. With a tenderness that belied the hunger in their gaze, they began to undress me, their fingers deftly undoing buttons and zippers, sliding fabric from skin until I stood naked before them, my body a canvas of desire painted with the flush of arousal.

The cool air of the room brushed against my exposed skin, causing me to shiver, though not from cold. My nipples pebbled, my breath came in short, shallow gasps, and a pulsing ache settled between my thighs.

Mark and Jen, still fully clothed, drank in the sight of me, their eyes traveling over every inch of my body. They seemed to relish the view, their gazes filled with appreciation and raw need. It was empowering, to be looked at in such a way—as if I were a work of art, a treasure to be savored.

Slowly, they began to undress, their movements synchronized, a sensual ballet performed for an audience of one. They revealed themselves to me, their bodies a testament to their mutual enjoyment of life's pleasures. Their clothes fell away, discarded in a heap on the floor, joining mine in a tangle of fabric.

They approached the bed, their naked forms a feast for my eyes. Mark was all lean muscle and restrained power, his member standing proud and ready. Jen was a vision of femininity, her curves an invitation to explore, her eyes alight with the same mischievous spark that had drawn me to her from the start.

They joined me on the bed, their bodies pressing against mine, a symphony of skin on skin, each touch a note in a melody of lust. We exchanged kisses, a cascade of sensation—lips on lips, lips on necks, lips on shoulders. It was a dance of desire, a mingling of breaths and sighs that set my nerves alight.

Then Mark's voice, a low growl in my ear. "Erika, would you like to experience more with a woman than just kisses?"

I nodded, my throat too tight with anticipation to speak.

Jen moved between my legs, her chestnut hair tickling my inner thighs. She started at my neck, her lips soft and insistent, leaving a trail of heat as she made her way down. Each kiss stoked the fire within me, a slow, tantalizing journey that had my back arching off the bed.

Her lips found my nipples, teasing them into hard peaks with her tongue and teeth. She lavished attention on my breasts, sending jolts of pleasure straight to my core. I writhed beneath her, my hands finding their way into her hair, pulling her closer, urging her on.

Jen's mouth continued its descent, her tongue tracing a path down my belly, every nerve ending singing with the promise of her touch. She reached my hips, her hands gripping my thighs, spreading them wider, opening me up to her gaze, her breath, her mouth.

She moved her head into position, her eyes locked on mine as she prepared to devour me. There was a moment of exquisite tension, a breath held in anticipation, and then...

As Jen's breath ghosted over my sensitive flesh, a shiver of anticipation rippled through me. Her eyes, dark with desire, held mine with an intensity that was both thrilling and unnerving. The room seemed to shrink until it was just the two of us, suspended in a moment of exquisite tension.

When her tongue finally made contact, it was a revelation. The soft, wet warmth against my aching center sent a jolt of pleasure through my body, causing me to gasp. Her movements were slow, deliberate, each stroke of her tongue a masterful caress that stoked the fire within me.

She traced the contours of my sex, her technique a mix of soft, teasing licks and firmer, insistent presses. She seemed to know instinctively how to unlock the growing need inside me, her mouth and tongue working in tandem to drive me wild with desire.

I could feel the slickness of my arousal, the evidence of how desperately I wanted this, how desperately I needed more. My fingers tangled in her hair, guiding her, urging her to increase her pace, to apply more pressure. But Jen was in control, her every movement a testament to her expertise and her desire to savor every moment.

As she delved deeper, her tongue exploring crevices I had forgotten could be so sensitive, I felt my control slipping. My hips bucked against her face, seeking more, my body moving of its own accord, driven by the primal rhythm of her ministrations.

The sensations were overwhelming, each lick, each suckle sending waves of pleasure crashing over me. My breath came in ragged gasps, my heart pounding in my chest like a wild drumbeat. I was lost in a sea of ecstasy, each wave carrying me higher, closer to the precipice of an orgasm that promised to be earth-shattering.

And then, just when I thought I could take no more, she slipped a finger inside me, curling it in a come-hither motion that hit a spot so deep, so intense, that it sent me spiraling. My entire body tensed, every muscle coiling tight as the orgasm ripped through me, a tsunami of pleasure that left me trembling, spent, and utterly sated.

As the waves of my climax began to ebb, Jen lifted her head, a triumphant smile playing on her lips. She crawled up my body, her skin slick against mine, and captured my mouth in a searing kiss. I could taste myself on her tongue, a heady reminder of the intensity of what we had just shared.

Mark, who had been watching with rapt attention, moved closer, his hand stroking my hair, his voice a low murmur in my ear. "You are so beautiful like this, Erika," he said, his words punctuated by the soft kisses he trailed down my neck. "So free, so uninhibited."

I turned to him, my eyes meeting his, conveying without words the gratitude and wonder I felt in this moment. He claimed my lips in a kiss that was both a benediction and a promise of pleasures yet to come.

The night was far from over, and as Jen nestled against my side and Mark's hands continued their exploration.

The aftershocks of my orgasm were still reverberating through my body when Mark's lips replaced Jen's, his tongue taking up the sweet torture where she had left off. The transition was seamless, a sensual relay where the baton was my pleasure.

Mark's approach was different—urgent, almost voracious, as if my release had awakened a primal hunger within him. His stubble scraped against my inner thighs, a delightful abrasion that contrasted with the softness of his tongue as it delved into my folds.

I was no stranger to the skill of a man's mouth, but Mark's technique was unlike anything I had experienced before. He seemed to intuitively understand the rhythm and pressure I needed, his tongue expertly flicking and circling my sensitive nub. Each stroke sent new jolts of electricity through my already oversensitized body, pushing me swiftly back to the brink of ecstasy.

Jen's hands roamed over my breasts, her fingertips teasing my nipples into hard peaks as she whispered words of encouragement into my ear. "That's it, Erika. Let go. Let us make you feel good."

The combination of their attentions was intoxicating. Mark's tongue was relentless, driving me higher and higher, while Jen's whispered affirmations filled my mind with images of unbridled passion and freedom. It was as if they were both determined to extract every last ounce of pleasure from my willing body.

I found myself clutching at the sheets, my body bowing off the bed as another orgasm began to build within me. It was a sensation so intense, so all-consuming, that it bordered on pain. But it was a pain I welcomed, a glorious burning that threatened to consume me whole.

And then it hit—a second climax that was even more powerful than the first. My vision blurred, my heart pounded, and a scream was torn from my throat as I was hurled into the abyss of pleasure. It was as if my body had been a tightly coiled spring, and now, with Mark's tongue as the catalyst, it was unleashed in a torrent of ecstasy.

As the last waves of my orgasm subsided, I lay there, limp and quivering, my breath coming in short, shuddering gasps. Mark lifted his head, his lips glistening with the evidence of my pleasure, and the pride in his eyes was unmistakable. He moved up to join us on the pillows, his arms encircling us both in a warm, satisfying embrace.

Jen, her eyes sparkling with a mix of satisfaction and excitement, pressed a soft kiss to my temple. "Welcome to our world, Erika," she murmured, her voice a sultry purr in the quiet of the room.

I turned to her, my gaze filled with gratitude and a new-found sense of belonging. This was more than just a physical encounter; it was a revelation, a reawakening of parts of me I had allowed to lie dormant for far too long.

Jen's voice, low and sultry, broke the languid silence that had settled over the room. She propped herself up on one elbow, her eyes locked on the sight of Mark's arousal, thick and straining against his belly.

"My, my," she purred, her gaze flicking up to meet mine, a mischievous glint in her dark eyes. "It seems my girl Erika here has worked my man up into quite the frenzy." She reached out, her fingers lightly tracing the length of him, and Mark let out a low groan, his hips arching up to meet her touch. "Care to help me take care of this little problem?"

The question hung in the air, a tantalizing invitation that sparked a surge of adrenaline through my veins. I watched as Jen's hand closed around Mark, her movements slow and deliberate, as if she were savoring the feel of him.

I felt a flush of heat rise to my cheeks as I realized what she was asking. The idea of participating in such an intimate act with another woman was thrilling and more than a little daunting. But the desire in Jen's eyes and the anticipation etched across Mark's face were impossible to resist.

With a nod, I reached out, my hand tentatively brushing against Jen's as we both gripped Mark's shaft. The sensation of his hot, hard length beneath our combined touch sent a jolt of arousal through me. I watched, fascinated, as our hands moved in unison, stroking him with long, languid movements that had him panting and arching off the bed.

As we worked together, I found myself getting caught up in the rhythm of our movements, the slick sounds of our hands on his skin, the intoxicating scent of sex that permeated the air. It was a symphony of the senses that had my own arousal spiking.

Jen leaned in, her breath hot against my ear. "Relax, Erika," she whispered. "Just let yourself feel."

I closed my eyes, allowing myself to get lost in the moment. Our hands continued their ministrations, our movements growing more confident, more purposeful as we explored the contours of Mark's body.

Suddenly, Mark's hand closed over mine, stilling our movements. His eyes, dark with desire, met mine. "I need to be inside you," he rasped, the urgency in his voice making my heart skip a beat.

Without a word, I straddled him, my body trembling with anticipation. Jen, ever the silent orchestrator of our pleasure, positioned herself in front of me, straddling Marks face her hands roaming over my hips, my breasts. She was a comforting presence, her touch grounding me even as it stoked the fire within.

As Mark entered me, a low moan escaped my lips. The feel of him inside me, combined with Jen's soft caresses, was almost too much to bear. It was a sensation overload, each thrust of Mark's hips, each stroke of Jen's hands sending me closer and closer to the edge.

Jen's lips found mine in a searing kiss that seemed to fuse our souls together. It was a kiss of shared passion, of mutual exploration, a testament to the bond that was forming between the three of us in this moment.

The rhythm of our bodies moving together was a dance as old as time, yet it felt entirely new to me. With each rise and fall of my hips, I could feel Mark's pleasure building, his moans of ecstasy vibrating against my core. I rode him with reckless abandon, my own desire fueled by the sight of Jen surrendering to her climax atop Mark's eager tongue.

Jen's body went rigid, her fingers digging into my flesh as she ground against Mark's face. Her cries of release filled the room, a symphony of pleasure that pushed me even closer to the edge.

As the last waves of her orgasm subsided, Jen dismounted, her body glistening with sweat, her eyes dark with lust.

She positioned herself beside us, her gaze locked on the sight of Mark's cock disappearing into my willing body. "Don't cum in her," she instructed him, her voice a throaty whisper that betrayed her own arousal. "I want to share it with Erika. I want us both to taste it. I want to taste her on your cock."

The thought of such an intimate act sent a shiver of anticipation through me. I had never tasted a man in such a way, let alone shared that experience with another woman. But in this moment, with Jen's dark eyes imploring me, it felt like the most natural thing in the world.

I nodded, my breath coming in short, sharp gasps as I continued to ride Mark. His hands gripped my hips, his fingers digging into my flesh as he fought to maintain control. I could feel the tension in his body, the way his muscles trembled with the effort of holding back his release.

Jen's hand reached out, her fingers tracing a path up my thigh, over my hip, until they brushed against my swollen clit. The contact was electric, sending a jolt of pleasure through my body that had me gasping. Her touch was light, teasing, a stark contrast to the pounding rhythm of our bodies.

"Come for us, Erika," she murmured, her fingers working their magic. "Let go and ride the wave."

Her words were my undoing. With a cry that seemed to come from the very depths of my soul, I felt my own climax crash over me. My body convulsed around Mark, my muscles clenching tight as wave after wave of pleasure washed over me.

As the last tremors of my orgasm subsided, I dismounted, my legs shaking with the aftermath of my release. Jen was there to catch me, her arms wrapping around me in a warm, reassuring embrace. Together, we turned our attention to Mark, who lay before us, his cock slick with the evidence of our shared passion.

Jen's eyes met mine, a silent question passing between us. With a nod, we both lowered our heads to the task at hand. Our tongues met in the middle, a tentative exploration that soon turned into a frenzy of desire as we tasted not just Mark, but each other.

The salty taste of Mark's arousal mingled with the sweetness of my own essence, a heady combination that had my pulse racing. I could feel Jen's excitement as she eagerly lapped at his length, her moans of pleasure vibrating against my lips.

It was a moment of pure, unadulterated hedonism, a celebration of the connection that the three of us shared. And as Mark finally reached his own shuddering climax, his release spilling onto our waiting tongues.

Mark's climax was a symphony of raw, unbridled passion. His body arched off the bed, his fingers tangling in our hair as he released himself into our shared embrace. His essence, warm and salty, filled our mouths, a tangible testament to the pleasure we had wrought.

Jen and I continued our dual assault on his cock, our tongues working in unison to coax every last drop from his trembling body. There was a primal satisfaction in this act, a sense of accomplishment that was both exhilarating and deeply intimate.

As Mark's shudders subsided and his body relaxed into the mattress, Jen turned to me. Her eyes, dark and luminous, held a question that needed no words. With a nod, I closed the distance between us, our lips meeting in a kiss that was both a surrender and a claiming.

The taste of Mark on Jen's tongue was an aphrodisiac, a potent mix of masculinity and submission that ignited a fresh surge of desire within me. We explored each other's mouths with a newfound fervor, sharing the evidence of our conquest. The kiss was deep and probing, a sensual dance that spoke of mutual respect and a hunger for more.

As our kiss deepened, I could feel Jen's excitement mirroring my own. Our bodies, slick with sweat and desire, moved together with a fluidity that spoke of hours spent in intimate exploration rather than mere minutes. It was as if we had been partners in passion for years, our movements attuned to the subtle cues and rhythms of each other's desires.

Eventually, we broke the kiss, our breaths coming in short, sharp gasps. We turned our gaze back to Mark, who lay spent and sated between us. A smile played on his lips, a silent acknowledgment of the pleasure we had delivered.

Jen reached out, her fingers lightly tracing the contours of Mark's chest. "That was incredible," she murmured, her voice thick with satisfaction. "You were incredible."

I nodded, my own words momentarily failing me. The experience had left me both exhilarated and humbled, a novice in the world of polyamory who had just been schooled in the art of shared pleasure.

The taste of Mark still lingered on my lips as I turned my attention to Jen. She lay beside him, her body flushed with the afterglow of our shared passion. Her dark eyes met mine, a silent invitation that set my pulse racing.

I had never experienced the taste of a woman prior to this moment, yet the desire burned within me, an imperative need.

With a boldness that surprised even me, I reached out, my hands sliding up her toned thighs to the apex of her legs. Her breath hitched as I gently nudged her apart, exposing the glistening folds of her sex to my hungry gaze.

I paused for a moment, taking in the sight of her—beautiful, wanton, and utterly open to me. The scent of her arousal was intoxicating, a musky perfume that seemed to call to something primal within me.

Slowly, almost reverently, I lowered my head between her legs. My tongue darted out, tentatively at first, as I explored her velvet softness. The taste of her was a revelation—sweet and salty, with an underlying hint of something uniquely Jen.

I heard her gasp as I found her clit, a small, hard nub that seemed to throb beneath my attentions. Encouraged by her response, I flicked my tongue over it, circling and teasing in a rhythm that soon had her writhing on the bed.

Beside us, Mark watched with heavy-lidded eyes, his hand lazily stroking his cock back to life. The sight of him, combined with the sounds of Jen's pleasure, spurred me on. I redoubled my efforts, my tongue delving deeper into her folds, eager to bring her the same mind-blowing pleasure she and Mark had given me.

Jen's fingers tangled in my hair, her hips bucking against my face as she climbed higher and higher. I could feel her body tense, her entire body tensing as she neared the precipice. With a final, desperate cry, she tumbled over the edge, her orgasm flooding my mouth with her essence.

I lapped at her gently, drawing out her pleasure until she lay spent and sated on the bed. Raising my head, I met her gaze, a sense of pride and satisfaction welling up within me. I had done this—brought her to the heights of ecstasy with my mouth, my tongue.

As I moved to sit up, Jen reached for me, pulling me into a searing kiss. The taste of our mingled desires on my lips seemed to ignite a fresh spark of desire in her, and I could feel the heat building between us once more.

Beside us, Mark groaned, his own arousal evident in the hard length of him. Jen turned to him, her eyes alight with mischief. "Your turn," she said, her voice a sultry promise that sent a shiver of anticipation through me.

Together, we descended upon him, our mouths and hands exploring every inch of his body. It was a dance of passion and desire, a celebration of the connection that the three of us shared. And as the night wore on, I knew that this was just the beginning of a journey of self-discovery and exploration that would change my life forever.

Chapter Twenty-One

The Morning After

I stumbled into my bathroom at 3 AM, legs still trembling from the hours spent with Mark and Jen. The woman in the mirror was a stranger—hair wild, lips swollen, eyes bright with something feral and unfamiliar. Purple marks bloomed across my collarbone and breasts, visible evidence of passion I couldn't erase.

The shower spray hit my skin, and I watched the evidence of our encounter swirl down the drain. My mind replayed fragments in disjointed flashes: Jen's mouth on mine, Mark's hands gripping my hips, the three of us tangled in a configuration I'd never imagined myself in. The physical sensations had been overwhelming, but now, alone with my thoughts, something else crept in.

I scrubbed harder, as if soap could wash away the tangle of emotions rising within me. Pride at my boldness mingled with disbelief. Who was this woman who'd done these things? Certainly not Erika Lawrence, mother of two, wife of Michael, part-time bookkeeper who volunteered at school fundraisers.

My hands shook as I toweled off. I'd crossed a line tonight that felt significant. Not just the physical act of being with two people simultaneously, but something deeper—a psychological boundary I hadn't known existed until I'd breached it.

I crawled into bed, careful not to wake Michael, my body aching pleasantly while my mind raced uncomfortably. The high of the experience was fading, leaving behind questions I wasn't ready to answer. What was I searching for in these increasingly extreme encounters? The validation and desire I'd initially craved seemed insufficient explanation for where I now found myself.

Sleep evaded me. I reached for my phone, opening my secret diary app. The clinical detachment of my previous entries was absent as I typed:

Dear Diary,

I don't recognize myself anymore. Tonight crossed into territory I never thought I'd explore. The physical pleasure was undeniable, but afterward... emptiness. A hollow space that expands with each new encounter. I'm chasing something that keeps moving further away.

I stared at the words, my finger hovering over the delete button. Acknowledging the emptiness made it real. Instead, I closed the app without saving.

CHAPTER TWENTY-TWO

The Secret Space

The morning after the threesome, I jolted awake with a horrifying realization. I'd left my dating app open on my phone. My stomach clenched as I frantically checked—relief flooding me when I saw the screen was locked. But the close call lingered like a warning.

Later that day, while the house was empty, I sat at my desk scrolling through my message history with growing unease. What if Zach or Lily borrowed my phone? What if Michael glanced over while I was typing? The spreadsheet documenting my encounters sat in a folder labeled "Budget Templates"—hiding in plain sight, protected by nothing but Michael's disinterest in household finances.

This wasn't sustainable. I needed a system—something foolproof.

At the electronics store that afternoon, I purchased a tablet with cash. The sales associate tried engaging me about features and warranty options, but I cut the conversation short. This device had one purpose only, and it wasn't family movie night.

"Gift for my niece," I explained with a practiced smile. The lie slipped out easily—another disturbing realization.

At home, I set up the tablet using a new email address, downloading all my dating apps and creating a secure password manager. I wiped my phone clean of any evidence, deleting apps and clearing browser history. The relief was immediate—a digital compartmentalization of my secret life.

But where to hide the tablet? The house suddenly felt transparent, lacking any truly private space. I scanned my home office, eyes landing on the deep bottom drawer of my desk.

That weekend, I visited a hardware store two towns over. I purchased a thin sheet of wood, wood glue, and small brass pulls. Back home, I emptied the drawer, measuring carefully. With precise cuts, I created a false bottom that fit snugly inside, leaving a hidden compartment beneath.

I tested it repeatedly—the false bottom holding firm when pulled, revealing the secret space only when pressed in a specific corner. Inside this compartment, I placed my tablet, a prepaid debit card I'd been using for hotels, and a small notebook containing information too sensitive to trust to digital storage.

Standing back, I surveyed my handiwork. The system felt secure, professional—evidence of how methodical I'd become in managing my double life.

The heatwave hit mid-July with brutal intensity. I woke to stifling air and damp sheets clinging to my skin. The ceiling fan spun uselessly overhead, pushing hot air in circles.

"Thermostat says it's eighty-four degrees in here," Michael said, his dress shirt already showing sweat stains as he knotted his tie. "AC must've died overnight."

I pulled my hair into a messy bun, already feeling dizzy from the heat. "Can you call someone before you leave?"

Michael made the call while I fixed breakfast for the kids. His frustrated sighs told me everything before he even hung up.

"Earliest they can come is Thursday. Everyone's backed up with this heatwave."

"Thursday? That's two days from now!" I glanced at the kitchen thermometer—already eighty-seven degrees and climbing.

"I'll pick up some window units after work." He kissed my forehead absently. "Try to stay cool."

After he left, the house became an oven. By noon, I couldn't focus on anything. Sweat trickled between my breasts as I paced the house, opening windows that only let in more hot air.

"The fans," I suddenly remembered. "The portable ones from the apartment."

In our first tiny apartment, we'd survived summer with three industrial-strength fans Michael's father had given us. They were noisy but powerful—and I was certain we'd stored them in the attic when we moved.

I pulled down the attic stairs, grimacing as a wave of even hotter air descended. Climbing up with a flashlight, I navigated through the maze of labeled boxes. Christmas decorations. Halloween. Winter clothes. Baby items I couldn't bear to part with.

Near the back, I spotted a box labeled "Apartment Stuff" in Michael's handwriting. I pushed aside a tower of plastic tubs containing Zach's outgrown sports equipment. As I shifted a heavy box of yearbooks and photo albums, something caught my eye—a large black container partially hidden behind the Christmas tree box.

Unlike everything else in our meticulously labeled attic, this container had no marking. It wasn't one of our regular storage bins either—this was a heavy-duty lock box type container with metal clasps. It looked deliberately tucked away behind the seasonal decorations where it wouldn't be casually discovered.

I hesitated. The container wasn't locked, just secured with two metal clasps. This was Michael's private box, hidden away. But wasn't I entitled to know what secrets my husband kept?

My fingers trembled as I unlatched the clasps. Inside lay a collection of items neatly arranged—photos, cards, and various mementos. Not the disorganized junk I expected, but carefully preserved memories.

I lifted out a stack of photographs. Michael, younger and more carefree, standing with friends I'd never met at what looked like a cabin by a lake. Another showed him raising a glass in a dimly lit bar, his arm around someone cropped from the picture.

Beneath the photos lay several greeting cards—birthday wishes, congratulations on promotions—signed with unfamiliar names. Nothing alarming, just pieces of a life he'd never shared with me.

Then I found it—a movie ticket stub. Next to it, a dinner receipt from Giovanni's, an upscale Italian restaurant in Chicago. I froze, my heart hammering against my ribs.

Michael had been in Chicago that weekend a couple of years ago—supposedly for a financial planning conference. I remembered the phone calls, his distracted voice as he described boring presentations and networking events.

Beneath the receipt lay a business card. "Alex Jenkins, Financial Consultant" with a Chicago address. A phone number was handwritten on the back—not a business number, but a personal one with a note: "Call anytime."

My mind raced back to that weekend. Michael had mentioned meeting "Alex" during the conference—a brilliant analyst he'd connected with professionally. I'd never questioned it. Why would I?

But now...

I stared at the evidence in my trembling hands. The intimate dinner. The movie. The personal number.

Alex. Alexandra? Alexis?

A hot flush of anger swept through me, followed immediately by a wave of perverse relief. If Michael had been unfaithful—was still being unfaithful—then was what I had been doing, really so wrong?

The secret rendezvous, the hidden communications, the fabricated business trips... My behavior mirrored his. We were both living double lives, seeking outside what we couldn't find at home.

I carefully replaced everything exactly as I'd found it, securing the clasps and returning the container to its hiding place. The fans lay forgotten as I descended the attic stairs, my mind whirling with justifications and rationalizations.

———◆———

Dear diary,

Maybe we're both living lies. Maybe that's what marriage becomes.

Found Michael's secret box today. Movie tickets, dinner receipt from that Chicago "conference" a couple of years ago. Business card for someone named Alex Jenkins with a personal phone number.

My hands are still shaking. All this time I've been drowning in guilt while he's been... what? Having his own affair? Meeting this Alex person on fake business trips?

The worst part is how relieved I felt. Like finding out your opponent in a game has been cheating all along, so your own cheating doesn't count anymore. Except this isn't a game. It's our marriage. Our family.

I keep thinking about how we got here. When did we stop talking? When did secrets become easier than the truth? I've created this elaborate double life, and apparently so has he. We pass each other in the kitchen, exchange pleasantries about the broken air conditioner, while carrying these hidden worlds inside us.

Maybe this is just what happens. The passion fades, the secrets grow, and you find yourself keeping score in a competition neither of you acknowledged entering.

I didn't confront him. What could I say without revealing my own infidelity? "I found evidence of your affair while I was scheduling my next hookup"?

We're mirrors now, reflecting each other's deceptions back and forth until the original image is lost completely. I don't even know who I am anymore. Mother, wife, secret seductress, betrayed spouse—all these versions of me exist simultaneously, fragmenting a little more each day.

Tomorrow I plan on getting out of this heat and finding a different kind of heat. I want...No I NEED to find a new cock to help me clear my mind. I should just stay at home. I know I should. But now there's this bitter justification fueling me. Why should I be the only one to sacrifice? Why should I feel guilty when he clearly doesn't?

Is this what the next decade looks like? Separate lives under one roof, maintaining appearances while we seek fulfillment elsewhere?

I used to think I knew what love was. Now I'm not sure I even know what marriage is anymore.

CHAPTER TWENTY-THREE

Stranger Danger

The bar was a pulsing vein of inebriated bodies, each one a potential escape from the stifling heat of her life. Erika couldn't even blame the broken air conditioner anymore. The heat was inside her now, a fever that no appliance could fix.

She sipped her drink, eyes scanning the crowd, not for the familiar, but for the unknown. It didn't take long. He was tall, dark hair peppered with silver, a shadow of stubble accentuating the strong line of his jaw. He moved with a quiet confidence that spoke of experience, his eyes meeting hers with an intensity that made her heart skip.

They exchanged names, but his was lost in the thrum of the music, or perhaps she never truly heard it. It didn't matter. He wasn't a person to her, but a vessel for her frustrations, her desires, her need to reclaim some semblance of power.

Their conversation was a dance of innuendos and knowing smiles. His hand found the small of her back, a possessive touch that sent shivers down her spine. When he leaned in to whisper in her ear, the heat of his breath against her skin was a stark contrast to the cool detachment she'd felt at home.

They left the bar together, the city lights a blur of colors reflecting off the wet pavement. His car was a sleek, dark sanctuary, parked just around the corner. Inside, the world seemed to shrink until it was just the two of them, wrapped in the heavy cloak of desire.

His hands were urgent, exploring her body with a hunger that matched her own. She should have cared about protection, about consequences, but in that moment, she felt invincible. The risk was part of the thrill, a way to lash out against the life that had caged her.

The windows fogged as they moved together, the rhythm of their bodies a wordless conversation that needed no vetting, no safeguards. It was raw and reckless, and when it was over, they sat in silence, the gravity of their actions hanging in the air between them.

Erika felt a mix of exhilaration and shame. She had once again crossed a line she could never uncross. And yet, as she stepped out of the car, her resolve hardened. If Michael was living a lie, why shouldn't she? If her marriage was a sham, why shouldn't she take what she needed from the world?

She walked away without a backward glance, the night air cool against her flushed skin. The risk she had taken was a stark reminder of how far she had fallen, but it also fueled a sense of defiance. She was no longer just a neglected wife or a mother trying to keep her family afloat. She was a woman on the edge, embracing the dangerous freedom that came with having nothing left to lose.

Dear diary,

I don't recognize myself anymore. The woman who drove home tonight isn't the same person who packed lunches this morning. My hands are still shaking as I write this.

I didn't even ask his name. I didn't want to know it. There's a strange power in anonymity—like if the person remains faceless, then what I've done somehow doesn't fully count. But it counts. God, it counts.

No protection. Not even a conversation about it. What am I doing? I have children. A life. Responsibilities. And yet I climbed into a stranger's car like a reckless teenager, except teenagers have the excuse of inexperience. What's mine? A broken air conditioner? A box in the attic with movie stubs?

I should feel disgusted with myself. I should be terrified of diseases, pregnancy, violence—all the dangers my mother warned me about. Instead, I keep replaying it in my mind, that moment when caution evaporated and there was nothing but sensation.

This isn't about Michael anymore. I can't even pretend it is. This is something else, something hungry inside me that won't be satisfied. Each encounter needs to be more dangerous than the last to give me that same rush. Like a drug that keeps requiring a higher dose.

I should stop. I will stop.

But even as I write those words, I know they're lies. I'm already thinking about tomorrow, about which app I'll check first, about what story I'll tell to carve out an hour of freedom.

What happens when an hour isn't enough? When do I cross the line from secret encounters to full-blown destruction of everything I've built?

I used to judge women like me. Now I am one.

The worst part isn't even the guilt. It's that beneath the guilt, buried under layers of shame and fear, is anticipation. Excitement for the next time. The next stranger. The next risk.

I need to sleep. Zach has a soccer game tomorrow, and Lily needs help with her science project. I'll wash my face, brush my teeth, and crawl into bed beside my husband. I'll play the role of devoted wife and mother.

Until the next time the heat rises and I need to escape.

CHAPTER TWENTY-FOUR

The Warning

The diner's noon rush surrounded us with background noise—just enough to mask our conversation from neighboring tables. Natalie hadn't touched her salad, just kept turning her water glass in slow circles, leaving condensation rings on the laminate tabletop.

"When's the last time you saw your kids' homework?" She dropped the question without preamble.

I blinked. "What?"

"Or asked Michael about his day? Or even showed up to book club?" She leaned forward. "I've been covering for you for three weeks. Three weeks, Erika."

The Caesar salad in my mouth turned to sawdust. I forced myself to swallow.

"I'm worried about you." Her voice softened. "This isn't just fun and games anymore. You've got that look—the same one my brother had before rehab."

"I'm not on drugs," I snapped.

"No. You're on something worse." She reached across the table and grabbed my hand. "Whatever hole you're trying to fill, these men aren't going to fill it."

I tried to pull away, but she held tight.

"You're taking crazy risks. Unprotected sex? With strangers? The Erika I know wouldn't do that."

Heat flashed across my face. "How did you—"

"You told me. Last Thursday. You were half-drunk and bragging about it like it was some achievement."

I had no memory of this conversation. The realization sent ice through my veins.

"I love you too much to watch you self-destruct." Her eyes welled up. "And those kids of yours? They need their mother. The real one, not this... whoever you're becoming."

"You encouraged me! You told me to explore!"

"A fling. Maybe two. Not turning your life into some secret sex tour." She shook her head. "There's exploring and then there's this... obsession."

The truth of her words landed like a physical blow. I stared at my half-eaten lunch, unable to meet her eyes.

"I'm scared for you, honey." Her voice cracked. "What happens when Michael finds out? Or when someone decides to follow you home? Or when you catch something that antibiotics can't fix?"

I pulled my hand away from Natalie's grip, straightening my shoulders.

"I'm in control. I know exactly what I'm doing." The words came out clipped, defensive.

Natalie's eyebrows shot up. "Really? Because from where I'm sitting, it looks like you're spiraling."

"You don't understand." I lowered my voice, leaning forward. "For the first time in years, I feel alive. Do you know how long I've been invisible? How long I've been just... existing?"

"And this is your solution? Anonymous hookups with men who don't even know your real name?"

I stabbed at my salad, skewering a crouton. "I have a system. I'm careful."

"Careful?" She laughed, but there was no humor in it. "You just told me about a guy whose name you don't even know."

"That was one time." The lie slipped out easily. "And I'm not stupid. I got tested last week." Another lie. I made a mental note to actually do it.

Natalie sighed, her shoulders slumping. "What about Michael? Your marriage?"

"What about it?" I felt a flash of righteous anger. "He checked out years ago. And after what I found in the attic—"

"What did you find?"

I waved my hand dismissively. "It doesn't matter. The point is, he's not exactly the devoted husband you think he is."

"So this is... what? Revenge?"

"No." I took a sip of water, gathering my thoughts. "It's reclaiming something that's mine. My body. My pleasure. My choices."

"At what cost, Erika?"

"I know my limits." I set my glass down with finality. "I appreciate your concern, but I'm fine. Better than fine, actually. I've never felt more in control."

The irony of that statement was lost on me then—how I was rearranging my entire life around these encounters, how I was lying to everyone I loved, how I'd started measuring time by the space between meetings.

"I can stop anytime I want," I added, the addict's classic refrain. "I just don't want to yet."

Natalie's face hardened. "That's exactly what my brother said. Right before he lost his job, his wife, and almost his life."

"I'm not your brother." I slammed my fork down. "And I'm not some addict you need to save."

"No? Then delete the apps. Right now." She held out her hand. "Show me your phone."

"Are you serious?"

"Completely." Her eyes narrowed. "If you're so in control, prove it."

My fingers curled around my purse strap. "I don't have to prove anything to you."

"That's what I thought." She sat back, arms crossed.

"You know what? You're just jealous." The words flew out before I could stop them. "You've been divorced for three years, and you're still bitter that I have options you don't."

Natalie's face went white. "Options? Is that what you call destroying your family?"

"That's not—"

"No, let me finish." She leaned forward, voice dropping to a fierce whisper. "You think I'm jealous? I'm terrified for you. This isn't some rom-com where you have a sexual awakening and everything works out. This is real life, where actions have consequences."

"Don't lecture me about consequences." I grabbed my purse. "You encouraged this. You planted the seed."

"And I regret it every day." Her voice cracked. "I never thought you'd take it this far."

"Well, I did. And I'm not stopping." I stood up, tossing a twenty on the table. "I thought you of all people would understand."

"I understand addiction when I see it." She didn't stand, just looked up at me with eyes full of disappointment. "And I can't watch you self-destruct anymore."

"Then don't." I turned to leave, then stopped. "And while you're sitting in judgment, remember who told me to 'get mine' in the first place."

"Erika—"

"No. I'm done being made to feel ashamed for finally putting myself first."

I walked out, ignoring the stares from neighboring tables, ignoring the fact that my only confidante was now sitting alone in a diner, ignoring the voice in my head that whispered she might be right.

CHAPTER TWENTY-FIVE

Family Suspicions

I slammed the front door harder than intended, the house empty except for the echo of my own anger. The fight with Natalie replayed in my head as I dropped my purse on the counter.

"Mom? Is that you?"

I startled at Lily's voice. She stood in the kitchen doorway, wearing oversized pajama pants despite it being mid-afternoon. Her dark hair—so like Michael's—was pulled into a messy bun, her eyes wary.

"Hey, sweetie. I thought you were at Kayla's." I forced a smile, trying to smooth the tension from my face.

"I came home early. Her mom got a migraine." She shifted her weight, studying me with that perceptive gaze that always made me feel transparent. "Are you okay? You look upset."

"Just traffic." I busied myself with the mail, avoiding her eyes. "Nothing important."

Lily didn't move. When I finally looked up, she was biting her lower lip—a nervous habit she'd had since childhood.

"Mom, can I ask you something?"

My stomach tightened. "Of course."

She took a deep breath. "Is everything okay? Between you and Dad, I mean."

The question hung in the air like smoke. I gripped the counter edge.

"Why would you ask that?"

She shrugged, but there was nothing casual about it. "You guys barely talk anymore. And when you do, it's like... I don't know. Like you're reading from scripts."

I swallowed hard. "Marriage has ups and downs, Lil. We're just busy."

"Dad sleeps in his office a lot." Her voice was quiet. "I hear him come upstairs really late, and sometimes he doesn't come up at all."

"He has deadlines." The excuse sounded hollow even to me.

"And you're gone all the time now. With work stuff or whatever." She made air quotes around "work stuff," and my heart stuttered. "It just feels different. Like something's wrong."

I crossed the kitchen and took her hands in mine. They were cold.

"Listen to me. Your father and I are fine. Every marriage goes through phases where things aren't perfect. That doesn't mean anythings wrong."

She searched my face. "Promise?"

I nodded, the lie burning my throat. "Promise."

"Okay." She didn't sound convinced. "It's just... Maddie's parents got divorced last year, and she said they acted exactly like you guys before they told her."

I watched Lily shuffle back to her room, her shoulders hunched in a way I'd never noticed before. The weight of her words crushed something inside me.

In the kitchen's silence, I sank onto a barstool. My phone buzzed with a notification from one of the apps. I turned it face down without looking.

When had I last really seen my children? Not just existed in the same space, but truly seen them? Zach's basketball season had started weeks ago. Had I attended a single game? And Lily—when had her eyes started carrying that adult worry?

I moved to the refrigerator where their school schedules used to be prominently displayed. The magnets remained, but the papers were gone. When had I stopped keeping track?

The house felt suddenly foreign, as if I'd been absent far longer than just a few hours. Evidence of my disconnection appeared everywhere I looked—a stack of permission slips I'd hastily signed without reading, a calendar with Zach's orthodontist appointment that I'd completely forgotten last week.

My gaze caught on a framed photo from last summer—the four of us at the lake, smiling. I remembered taking that picture but couldn't recall the conversations we'd had that day. What had Lily been excited about? What story had Zach told that made Michael laugh so hard?

I pulled out my tablet from its hiding place and stared at the screen. Three unread messages from men whose faces I could barely distinguish from one another. Men who knew nothing about me—not my children's names, not my actual birthday, not a single thing that mattered.

What was I doing? While I'd been constructing elaborate fantasies and chasing hollow thrills, my daughter had been watching her family disintegrate, piecing together adult concerns no thirteen-year-old should have to carry.

I thought I'd been invisible to everyone. But my children had seen me all along—seen the absences, the distraction, the growing distance. They'd been watching as I vanished, not just from my marriage, but from them.

I slid the tablet into its hiding place, tucking it beneath the false bottom drawer I'd installed. My fingers lingered on its smooth surface before I snapped the compartment shut. The conversation with Lily had shaken me, but not enough to make me want to stop.

I just needed to be smarter. More careful.

In the bathroom, I splashed cold water on my face and stared at my reflection. The woman looking back had changed—her eyes held secrets, her lips curved with newfound confidence despite the guilt lurking beneath.

"You can have both," I whispered to myself. "You just need better boundaries."

I pulled out my phone and deleted the dating apps that sent notifications. I'd reinstall them later on the tablet only. No more lunchtime meetups—too risky with my erratic schedule raising questions. No more local hotels where I might run into someone I knew.

I created a mental checklist: drive at least thirty minutes away for any encounter. Use cash whenever possible. Develop better cover stories. Pay more attention to the kids when I was home to compensate for my absences.

I needed to be present enough that no one would question when I wasn't.

Opening my calendar, I blocked out time for Zach's next three basketball games and added a reminder to ask Lily about her art project. I'd show up for breakfast every morning, help with homework in the evenings. I'd rebuild the façade of normal family life while carefully carving out space for my other needs.

The solution seemed so obvious now. I didn't have to choose between my family and my freedom. I just had to manage both worlds better, keep them from bleeding into each other.

I picked up my phone again and texted Natalie: "You were right. I'm being more careful from now on."

What I didn't add was that "being careful" didn't mean stopping. It just meant covering my tracks better, compartmentalizing more effectively. Creating a perfect system where I could live both lives without anyone getting hurt.

It was a lie I desperately needed to believe.

CHAPTER TWENTY-SIX

The Business Trip

"A whole week?" I echoed, watching Michael pack his suitcase with meticulous precision. "That's longer than usual."

"Big client in Seattle. If we land this account, it could mean that promotion I've been after." He folded another dress shirt along invisible lines. "The timing's not ideal with the kids' schedules, but I can't pass this up."

I nodded, careful to maintain the right balance of supportive wife and mildly inconvenienced mother. "We'll manage. When do you leave?"

"Sunday afternoon. Back late the following Sunday." He paused, looking up from his packing. "You sure you'll be okay with everything? Zach has that tournament next weekend."

"I've got it covered." The plans were already forming, possibilities unfurling like a map of unexplored territory. Seven nights. Six full days. No need to rush home, no excuses needed for late nights.

Michael zipped his suitcase closed. "I'll make it up to you when I get back. Maybe we could go away for a weekend, just us?"

"That would be nice," I said, the words hollow in my mouth.

After he left the room, I pulled out my tablet from its hiding place. Seven nights of freedom stretched before me like an empty canvas. I could reinvent myself each evening, become someone new with each sunset. No rushed encounters, no checking the time, no hurrying home to maintain appearances.

I opened one of the dating apps and began scrolling, already categorizing potential matches into different nights. Monday could be the silver-haired executive who'd been messaging for weeks. Wednesday perhaps the visiting professor from Boston. The weekend held more possibilities—maybe even an overnight stay somewhere, waking up beside a stranger without the panic of morning schedules.

My fingers hovered over the screen, heart racing with anticipation. This wasn't just opportunity—it was liberation. A full week to explore every fantasy without constraint.

I created a new note titled "Seattle Week" and began planning with the same precision Michael had shown packing his suitcase. Each day mapped out, each alibi crafted, each potential encounter vetted. This would be my week of total freedom, and I intended to use every minute of it.

The week unfolded with a rhythm both exhilarating and terrifying. Each day dawned with a frisson of anticipation, a thrumming undercurrent to the mundane routine of motherhood and domesticity. With Michael gone, I was the captain of my own ship, charting a course through uncharted waters.

Monday's executive turned out to be a man of few words and many talents. We met at a hotel bar downtown, the anonymity of the place making my heart flutter with dangerous excitement. The lobby was a blur of suits and business jargon, the perfect backdrop for our clandestine rendezvous. He was older, his hands sure and confident as they guided me through the hotel's corridors to a room he'd booked under a false name. There was an urgency to our coupling, a rawness that left me breathless and shaking. The risk of being caught in such a public place heightened every sensation, turning casual glances in the hallway into potential discoveries that thrilled and terrified me in equal measure.

Tuesday's professor was a departure from the weekend's intensity. We met in the quiet corner of a library, surrounded by the scent of old books and the soft shuffling of patrons. Our conversation was a dance of intellect and innuendo, each word a step closer to the inevitable. When we finally gave in to our desires, it was in the stacks, hidden amongst the shadows and silence.

The air in the library was thick with the musk of aged paper and hushed whispers. The professor's eyes, a startling shade of green, held a hunger that matched my own. I had met him only an hour ago, yet here I was, surrendering to the forbidden thrill of the moment.

I stood before him, the weight of my decision pressing against my chest. He reached out, his fingers tracing the line of my jaw, gentle yet insistent. My breath hitched as he tugged at my lower lip, his thumb lightly grazing the sensitive skin.

In the dim light of the library, amidst the echoes of silence, I felt the familiar pull of desire low in my belly. It was a craving that had grown more insistent with each passing encounter, a yearning for something beyond the safety of my marriage, beyond the predictability of my life.

With a boldness that surprised even me, I dropped to my knees before him, the plush carpet of the library a soft cushion beneath me. My hands found the hem of his trousers, fumbling slightly as I worked to free the stiff cock that strained against the fabric.

He let out a low groan as I wrapped my fingers around him, feeling the heat of his arousal through the thin material of his boxers. His hand came to rest on my head, guiding me closer, urging me on with a quiet intensity that left no room for hesitation.

I pulled down his boxers, and his cock sprang free, thick and hard and pulsing with need. A thrill of power coursed through me at the sight of him, at the knowledge that I was the one who had brought him to this state of aching desire.

With a soft exhale, I took him into my mouth, the salty taste of his skin on my tongue mingling with the musty scent of the books that surrounded us. His hips bucked slightly at the sensation, and I heard him stifle a moan, the sound muffled by the oppressive quiet of the library.

I moved slowly at first, savoring the feel of him against my lips, the way his breathing grew ragged and uneven as I explored him with my tongue. His fingers tightened in my hair, pulling gently, guiding my rhythm as I began to move faster, taking him deeper with each stroke.

The world around us faded into a haze of lust and longing, the only reality the sound of our breaths and the pulsing of his cock in my mouth. I was lost in the moment, consumed by the need to please him, to push him over the edge and into the abyss of pleasure that awaited us both.

The thought of being caught aroused me and spurred me on. Every footstep in the adjacent aisle sent electric currents through my body. The danger heightened everything—his taste, his scent, the way his fingers tangled in my hair as I took him deeper. Each approaching sound made me work faster rather than pull away.

"Someone's coming," he whispered, his voice strained.

I didn't stop. Couldn't stop. The possibility of discovery had become part of the thrill, a necessary component of my pleasure. My heart hammered against my ribs as the footsteps grew closer, the rhythmic squeak of library cart wheels approaching our secluded corner.

He tried to pull back, but I gripped his thighs, holding him in place. His eyes widened in shock, then darkened with understanding. This wasn't just about sex anymore—it was about pushing boundaries, about finding the edge of what was acceptable and leaping beyond it.

The cart paused at the end of our aisle. I heard the soft thud of books being reshelved, the librarian humming quietly to herself. She was mere feet away, separated only by a row of ancient encyclopedias. One step around the corner and she would see us—me on my knees, mouth full of his cock and him with his head thrown back in pleasure.

The proximity of discovery sent waves of heat through my body. My free hand slipped beneath my skirt, finding the wetness there, my body's response to the danger we courted. I worked myself in rhythm with my mouth on him, racing toward release with the soundtrack of potential catastrophe in my ears.

The librarian's cart squeaked again, moving closer. I locked eyes with the professor, saw the conflict there—the fear of exposure warring with the ecstasy of the moment. But I didn't relent, driven by something primal and reckless that had taken root inside me.

As I felt him grow impossibly harder, I knew he was close. I redoubled my efforts, driven by a primitive urge to bring him to completion, to feel the rush of his release fill my mouth. With a final, shuddering moan, he came, his body tensing as wave after wave of ecstasy washed over him.

I instinctively swallowed, the taste of him a potent reminder of the power I held in that moment, a power that was both exhilarating and terrifying in its intensity.

As the aftershocks of his orgasm subsided, I slowly released him from my mouth, carefully tucking him back into his trousers with a tenderness that belied the raw passion of our encounter.

For a moment, we remained there, neither of us speaking, neither of us willing to break the spell that had been woven around us. Then, with a final, lingering look, I rose to my feet, my knees aching from the hard floor, my body humming with the remnants of our shared desire.

I had crossed another line, pushed another boundary, and yet, as I slipped away into the shadows of the library, I felt more alive than I had in years. This was my secret life, a tapestry of stolen moments and illicit pleasures, and I had no intention of turning back now.

The fear of being overheard added an edge to our encounter, the quiet whispers of our passion a stark contrast to the public setting.

Wednesday, I was chasing the high of risk with a reckless abandon. I found myself in the back of a cab with a stranger, the city lights a blur through the rain-spattered windows. The driver hummed along to a radio tune, oblivious to the illicit acts unfolding in his rearview mirror. The urgency of our encounter, the danger of being discovered by the driver or passing cars, lent an intensity to our connection that was as terrifying as it was intoxicating.

Thursday night, I threw caution to the wind. A chance meeting at a rooftop bar led to a spontaneous decision to follow a dark-eyed stranger into the night. We found an alleyway, the pulsing music from the bar spilling out into the cool night air. Our encounter was frenzied, fueled by the adrenaline of our public location. The possibility of being seen, the knowledge that anyone could stumble upon us at any moment, added a layer of danger that I had come to crave.

The beat of the music was a primitive drum that echoed the racing of my heart as I followed him into the shadows of the alleyway. My heels clicked on the asphalt, a staccato rhythm that seemed too loud, too conspicuous for our clandestine rendezvous. The rooftop bar, with its pulsing lights and raucous laughter, felt a world away as we slipped into the narrow strip of darkness between the buildings.

He moved with a quiet confidence, his dark eyes never leaving mine as he led me to a secluded spot behind a garbage dumpster. The smell of refuse filled the air, a stark contrast to the perfume and cologne that had mingled in the crowded bar. But the scent of decay didn't diminish the desire that coursed through my veins—if anything, it heightened the raw, animalistic nature of our encounter.

Without a word, I turned away from him, my body pressed against the cold brick wall of the alley. I gathered my skirt in my hands, pulling it up over my ass with a swift, practiced motion. The cool night air kissed my exposed skin, a shock of sensation that sent a shiver running down my spine.

I heard the rustle of fabric behind me, the sound as charged as a crack of thunder in the stillness of the night. He was quick, his movements driven by a fierce, unspoken need. His cock sprang free from the confines of his pants, hard and ready and throbbing with anticipation.

He didn't hesitate, didn't pause to savor the moment. There was no time for tenderness, no room for slow exploration. This was about raw, unadulterated desire, the kind that couldn't be contained or controlled.

With a low, guttural growl, he thrust into me furiously. I gasped as his cock filled me, the sharp sting of his entrance a stark contrast to the silken heat of his body against mine. My fingers scrambled for purchase against the rough bricks, the texture of the wall a stark contrast to the smooth, wet slide of his flesh against mine.

He moved with a wild abandon, each thrust driving me further into the wall, each snap of his hips a testament to the primal urgency of our coupling. The sound of our bodies coming together was a wet, rhythmic slap that echoed in the narrow confines of the alley, a dirty symphony that was as thrilling as it was forbidden.

I could feel the orgasm building within me, a tightening in my core that spiraled outwards with each brutal thrust. I closed my eyes, losing myself in the sensation of being taken, of being wanted with such ferocious intensity.

The danger of our exposure, the certainty that we could be discovered at any moment, only added to the frenzy of our encounter. There was a wildness to our passion, a ferocity that was as exhilarating as it was terrifying. We were two strangers, joined together in a moment of pure, unadulterated lust, our bodies speaking a language that required no words.

He reached around, his fingers finding my clit as he continued to thrust into me with reckless abandon. The dual sensation of his cock inside me and his fingers on me was driving me wild.

His movements became more erratic, his rhythm faltering as he chased his release. With a final, powerful thrust, he buried himself deep inside me, his body shuddering as he came. The feel of his cock pulsing within me was a potent reminder of the power of our connection, a fleeting moment of intimacy that transcended the physical.

We remained joined together, taking time to savor the moment, our harsh breaths the only sound in the otherwise silent alleyway. Then, with a reluctant sigh, he withdrew from me, tucking himself back into his pants with practiced ease.

The world narrowed to the pulsing ache between my legs, the echo of his release still reverberating through my body. My breath came in short, ragged gasps, the brick wall cool against my flush skin. I could feel the slickness of his spend trickling down my inner thigh, a stark reminder that while he had found his release, I was still a prisoner of my own unfulfilled desire.

He stepped back, his footsteps on the asphalt fading as he retreated into the night, leaving me trembling and unfulfilled in the shadowed alley. I could hear the muffled thump of the bar's music in the distance, the beat a dull throb in my chest. I was alone now, the thrill of our encounter giving way to a gnawing emptiness.

I closed my eyes, leaning my forehead against the wall, the rough texture grounding me amidst the swirl of my emotions. I needed more—more touch, more friction, more everything. My body was a taut wire, vibrating with pent-up need, the orgasm that had threatened to overwhelm me still out of reach.

I slipped my hand beneath the waistband of my underwear, my fingers slipping through the wetness there. I circled my clit with a light, teasing touch, each pass sending sparks of pleasure coursing through my veins. I bit my lower lip to stifle the moan that threatened to escape, the sound too dangerous in the open air of the alley.

My fingers moved faster, the pressure building with each slick slide. I could feel the walls of my pussy fluttering, the sensation threatening to pull me under. I imagined it was his hands on me, his fingers coaxing me toward release, the phantom touch fueling my desire.

I chased the elusive wave of my orgasm, my body a coiled spring, desperate for release. The world around me blurred at the edges, the sounds of the city fading into a distant hum as I focused solely on the pleasure that was building within me.

The frustration built within me, a tidal wave of unfulfilled desire that left me aching and unsatisfied. My fingers, slick with the evidence of my arousal, moved with a frantic urgency, but it wasn't enough—I needed more than the fleeting touches I could provide myself. I needed the weight of another body pressing me into the wall, the thrust of a hard cock inside me, the danger of being caught to push me over the edge.

I straightened my clothes and stepped out of the shadows of the alley, my body still throbbing with need. The night was young, and the city was alive with possibilities. I could feel the pulse of it beneath my feet, a siren song that called to the darker parts of my soul.

I made my way back to the bar, my heels clicking on the sidewalk, each step a silent promise to myself. I wouldn't go home unfulfilled, wouldn't allow the night to end in anything but ecstasy.

The bar was even more crowded now, the air thick with the scent of perfume and whiskey and the unmistakable tang of desire. I pushed my way through the throng of bodies, the heat of their collective warmth seeping into my skin, stoking the fire that raged within me.

I found a spot at the bar, my body humming with anticipation as I scanned the room for a potential partner. I needed someone who could match the intensity of my need, someone who wouldn't shy away from the raw, animalistic hunger that simmered just beneath the surface of my skin.

My gaze landed on a man sitting alone at a corner table, his eyes locked on mine with an intensity that took my breath away. He was handsome in a rugged, unrefined sort of way, with a day's worth of stubble on his jaw and a lock of dark hair that fell across his forehead.

I made my way over to him, my stride confident, my intentions clear. His eyes never left me as I approached, the heat in his gaze igniting a fresh wave of arousal that pulsed between my legs.

"Is this seat taken?" I asked, gesturing to the empty chair across from him.

He shook his head, a small smile playing at the corners of his mouth as he motioned for me to sit. "It's all yours," he said, his voice a low rumble that resonated somewhere deep within me.

I slid into the chair, my legs brushing against his under the table. The contact was electric, a jolt of pure, unadulterated lust that left us both breathless.

I leaned into him, my breath a warm whisper against his ear. "I was just fucked by another man in the alley," I murmured, my voice barely audible above the din of the bar. "He came inside me, but before I could... I need to cum. Do you think you could help a lady out?"

His sharp intake of breath was all the answer I needed. His hand found mine under the table, his fingers intertwining with mine in a silent promise of what was to come. "I'd be more than happy to assist," he said, his voice a low growl that sent a shiver of anticipation down my spine.

We didn't waste any time. He threw some money on the table, enough to cover our drinks and then some, a tip for the inconvenience of our sudden departure. We rose in unison, our bodies moving with a shared purpose, a mutual understanding of what was about to happen.

Together, we slipped out of the bar, our fingers intertwined, our bodies moving in sync as we stepped out into the night. The world around us seemed to blur, the sounds of the city fading into the background as we gave in to the desires that had been simmering between us.

We didn't make it far, the pull of our attraction too strong to ignore. We found a secluded spot behind a nearby building, the shadows providing a modicum of privacy in the bustling cityscape.

He pressed me against the wall, his body a solid weight against mine. His hands were everywhere, exploring, teasing, stoking the fire within me to a fever pitch.

I could feel his cock, hard and insistent against my hip, a tangible reminder of the pleasure that was to come. I reached for him, my fingers closing around the thick length of him, the silken heat of his skin a stark contrast to the cool night air.

With a low growl, he captured my mouth in a searing kiss, his tongue sliding against mine in a mimicry of the act we were both so desperate to perform. The taste of him was intoxicating, a potent mix of whiskey and desire that left me dizzy with need.

He hiked up my skirt, his fingers sliding beneath the waist-band of my underwear to find the wetness that awaited him. I moaned into his mouth as he plunged two fingers inside me, the sudden intrusion a welcome relief from the aching emptiness that had plagued me for hours.

He worked me with a practiced ease, his fingers moving in and out of my pussy with a rhythm that had me gasping for breath. I could feel the orgasm building within me, a tidal wave of pleasure that threatened to sweep me away.

But I needed more—needed the feel of his cock inside me, the connection that only skin-to-skin contact could provide.

With a swift, practiced motion, he freed himself from the confines of his pants. He positioned himself at my entrance, the broad head of his cock nudging against my swollen folds.

I wrapped my legs around his waist, pulling him closer, urging him on with a needy whimper that seemed to come from somewhere deep within me.

And then, with one powerful thrust, he was inside me, filling me, completing me in a way that I had desperately needed. He moved with a raw, unbridled passion, each snap of his hips driving me further and further toward the edge.

The world around us seemed to fall away, the only reality the feel of his body against mine, the sound of our ragged breaths echoing in the stillness of the night. His cock moving inside me with a relentless rhythm, each thrust pushing me closer to the release I so desperately craved.

I could feel the orgasm building within me, with each pounding stroke. My fingers dug into the muscles of his back, the pleasure coursing through my veins too intense to bear in silence.

With a final, shuddering cry, I came, the force of my orgasm washing over me in waves that left me breathless and spent. He followed, his body tensing as he found his own release, his cock pulsing inside me as he filled me with his warmth.

We remained there, our bodies joined together in the aftermath of our shared ecstasy. Then, with a reluctant sigh, he withdrew from me, tucking himself back into his pants.

I straightened my clothes, my body still humming with the aftershocks of my orgasm. I looked up at him, my eyes meeting his in the dim light of the alleyway.

"Thank you, I needed that." I whispered, the words a sincere expression of the gratitude I felt for the pleasure he had given me, for the escape he had provided from the relentless ache of my unfulfilled desire.

He simply smiled, a genuine, unguarded smile that lit up his entire face. "Anytime," he said, the warmth in his voice a stark contrast to the coolness of the night air.

And with that, I kissed his cheek and we parted ways, each of us stepping back into the anonymity of the city, our brief but intense connection nothing more than a memory that would linger long into the night.

I stepped out of the shadows of the alley, my heels clicking on the pavement as I made my way back to the world that awaited me beyond the seductive lure of my double life. The knowledge that I would return to this world of shadows and secrets was a certainty that filled me with both anticipation and a creeping sense of dread.

But for now, I was sated—a temporary reprieve from the relentless pursuit of my next high, my next encounter, my next escape from the life that I had once known as my own. I hailed a cab, the neon glow of the city lights painting the night in shades of desire and decadence, and for a moment, I allowed myself to bask in the quiet satisfaction of a craving fulfilled.

The rest of the week stretched before me, a canvas of possibility that both thrilled and terrified me. But for now, I allowed myself a moment of reprieve, a brief respite from the relentless pursuit of my next high.

I realized that I was playing a dangerous game. The thrill of the chase, the allure of the forbidden, had become an addiction I couldn't shake. Each rendezvous was a step further into the abyss, a leap into the unknown with no safety net to catch me. I was dancing on the edge of a blade, and with each encounter, I moved closer to the sharp, precarious tip.

Dear diary,

Conquests. Hotel bar downtown. Banker from Chicago. 35-40. Dark hair, athletic. Room 412. Quick, efficient. Left before he woke up.

Coffee shop pickup. Professor type. My car, back lot of the community college. His hands were soft. Too many questions afterward. Won't repeat.

Back-to-back day. Need to be careful. Dating app. Construction foreman. His truck. Rough in the best way. No names exchanged. Perfect.

Gym guy (not trainer). Followed me to changing room after hours. Risk of getting caught = incredible high. Must try similar scenario again.

Michael asked about my "glow" this morning. If only he knew. another was bartender after closing. Counter sex. Left my panties behind on purpose.

Two in one day. - Lunch break, hotel quickie with app match. - Evening bar stranger. Starting to lose track of faces. Just sensations now.

Another can't remember his job. Doesn't matter. Hotel again. Trying new positions helps keep it interesting. Need more variety.

Three-day gap. Too long. Irritable with kids. Another milestone! Celebrated with first outdoor encounter. Park after dark. Risk factor: 9/10.

Natalie's neighbor. She'd kill me if she knew. His eyes reminded me of Michael's. Didn't finish. Left abruptly.

Made up for previous disappointment. Two more today. Morning: gym trainer again. Evening: business traveler from dating app. Both delivered.

Another but I can't remember details. Was I drinking too much? Need to stay sharp. Control slipping?

CHAPTER TWENTY-SEVEN

The Party

I stared at the invitation glowing on my tablet screen. Private address in the upscale Lakeside district. "Exclusive gathering. Discreet attendees. Dress to impress." The message had come from a man I'd chatted with briefly—investment banker, divorced, impossibly handsome profile photo that I half-suspected was fake.

I shouldn't go. Anonymous hotel rooms and quick encounters were one thing. A party meant faces, names, connections. Risk.

But the risk made my heart race.

I pulled out a dress I'd bought during my reinvention phase—black, tight, with a neckline that plunged just enough to make Michael raise his eyebrows the one time he'd seen it hanging in my closet. I told him it was for a charity event and never wore it. Until tonight.

"Working late," I texted Michael. "Quarterly reports due tomorrow."

The Uber dropped me at a modernist mansion perched on a hillside overlooking the city. Security at the gate checked my name against a list. Inside, the space opened to floor-to-ceiling windows, sleek furniture, and beautiful people mingling with cocktails that glowed under recessed lighting.

I spotted my contact across the room. He was real—and even more striking in person. He approached with two martinis.

"Erika. You came." His voice was deep, cultured. "I wasn't sure you would."

I took the drink. "I surprise myself these days."

His eyes traveled down my body. "That makes two of us."

The crowd was eclectic—professionals mostly, ranging from thirties to fifties. Everyone attractive, polished. Everyone watching each other with hungry eyes.

"What exactly is this party?" I asked, though I was beginning to understand.

He leaned close, his breath warm on my ear. "A gathering of like-minded individuals. Everyone here is looking for something they can't find at home."

I should have felt shocked. Instead, I felt a thrill of recognition. These were my people now. Secret-keepers. Thrill-seekers.

"See anyone you like?" he asked, nodding toward the room. "The night is young, and options are... plentiful."

As I sipped my martini, a woman approached us—dark hair, red lips, a dress that left little to the imagination. She kissed my contact on the cheek, then turned to me with an appraising look.

"So, you're the enigmatic Erika?" she purred. "I'm Isabella."

I nodded, a bit taken aback by her directness. "Nice to meet you, Isabella."

She linked her arm with mine, drawing me away from the crowd. "Let me show you around," she said, her voice a sultry whisper meant only for me.

We wandered through the mansion, each room holding new surprises. A couple entwined on a velvet chaise, their clothes scattered on the marble floor. In a dimly lit library, a group was engaged in a tangle of limbs and soft moans. My cheeks flushed, but Isabella simply smiled, unfazed.

"This is a place of freedom," she said, leading me up a winding staircase. "No judgment. No inhibitions. Just... pleasure."

At the top, she opened a door to a room filled with plush pillows and draped silks. A man reclined on a loveseat, watching as a woman danced for him, her movements hypnotic and sensual.

Isabella's hand brushed mine. "You're curious," she said, not a question but a statement. "Why not indulge?"

I looked at her, then back at the scene before me. This was a world away from my life as Erika, the mother and wife. Here, I was a stranger, unshackled by my daily identity.

Feeling a surge of boldness, I stepped into the room. My heart pounded in my chest, a rhythm that matched the pulsing music filtering through hidden speakers.

"Join us," the man on the loveseat beckoned, his eyes locked on mine.

I hesitated for a moment, then set my drink down and let the music guide my movements. The woman dancing showed me how to let go, how to move in a way that felt both ancient and entirely new.

In the background, I heard Isabella's throaty laugh, a sound of pure enjoyment. "That's it," she encouraged. "Lose yourself in it."

As I danced, the room seemed to shift around me. Faces blurred, conversations became a distant hum, and all that mattered was the music and the heat of bodies around me.

When the song ended, the room erupted in applause. I stood there, breathing heavily, my skin alive with sensation.

The man on the loveseat rose and approached me, his gaze intense. "May I?" he asked, his hand extended.

I took it, feeling the thrill of anticipation. This was a crossroads, and I knew that whatever choice I made next would irrevocably alter the path I was on.

But for now, in this moment, I was exactly where I wanted to be.

The applause still echoing in my ears, I let the man lead me to the center of the room. His touch was confident, his eyes never leaving mine. The others watched, a circle of spectators that seemed to grow with each passing second.

He reached into a small wooden chest beside the loveseat and pulled out a mask—a delicate piece of lacquer and lace that covered the upper half of the face, leaving only the eyes visible.

"May I?" he repeated, this time holding up the mask.

I nodded, a silent agreement, and he gently secured it behind my head, his fingertips brushing against my neck. With the mask in place, I felt a sense of anonymity wash over me. I was no longer Erika, the wife and mother. I was a nameless reveler in a world designed for pleasure.

The music started again, slower this time, a sultry rhythm that seemed to seep into my bones. I began to move, the mask lending me a sense of boldness I'd never felt before. It was as if I'd shed my old skin, leaving behind all fears and insecurities.

The man watched me, his eyes dark with desire. He didn't approach, didn't reach out to touch me. Instead, he seemed content to observe, to drink in the sight of my masked form dancing just for him.

In the haze of the dimly lit room, others joined me. Hands, faceless and unknown, caressed my arms, my waist, my hair. I felt the heat of their bodies as they moved around me, a whirlwind of sensation and desire. I was an object of lust, yet I felt empowered, not diminished.

I danced with abandon, my body responding to the rhythm and the touches that came from every direction. It was a new level of depersonalization, a complete detachment from my everyday life. Here, I was free from the constraints of my identity, free from the expectations and disappointments that came with it.

The man who'd given me the mask finally approached, his movements fluid and graceful. He drew me close, his hand splayed across the small of my back, and we moved together as one. I could feel the contours of his body, the warmth of his skin through the thin fabric of his robe.

Our dance was intimate, a silent conversation between two souls unburdened by names or pasts. It was a connection that existed only in this room, in this moment, and it was intoxicating.

As the music swelled to a crescendo, he dipped me low, his lips grazing the exposed skin of my neck. A shiver ran down my spine, a visceral reaction to the electricity that sparked between us.

When the song ended, we stood there, chests heaving, our breaths mingling beneath the mask that still concealed my identity. The room erupted in applause once more, but this time, it was just a backdrop to the pounding of my heart.

The man gazed at me, a question in his eyes. I knew that if I stayed, the night would take me further down this path of hedonistic exploration.

The man's eyes held mine as he reached for the straps of my dress. With a deftness that spoke of experience, he slid them from my shoulders, the fabric whispering against my skin as it pooled at my feet. I stood before him—before them all—completely naked, my body illuminated by the soft, ambient lighting of the room.

A murmur of appreciation rippled through the onlookers, a chorus of anonymous admirers whose gazes caressed my exposed flesh. I felt a flush of heat rise to my cheeks, but it wasn't shame that colored my skin—it was the raw, undeniable thrill of being so thoroughly on display.

With a gentle hand, the man guided me to a large, ornately decorated pedestal that stood in the center of the room. It was covered in a plush velvet that felt cool against my overheated skin as he helped me lie back. He positioned himself between my legs, his gaze lingering on the most intimate part of me.

Slowly, he leaned forward, his intention clear. I gasped as his mouth made contact with my sensitive flesh, his tongue tracing a path along my folds with expert precision. He explored me with a hunger that left me breathless, each lick and suckle sending waves of pleasure through my body.

I arched into his touch, my hands finding their way into his hair, urging him on. The room around us faded into a hazy backdrop as I surrendered to the exquisite sensations coursing through me.

The man was relentless, his desire to please me evident in every movement of his tongue. I could feel the tension building within me, a crescendo of ecstasy that threatened to overwhelm my senses.

As the first waves of orgasm began to ripple through my body, I let out a moan that seemed to echo off the walls. The sound was swallowed by the room, lost amidst the murmurs of the crowd that had gathered to watch the spectacle.

My climax hit me with the force of a tidal wave, my body convulsing with the intensity of my release. The man held me firmly, his mouth never leaving my quivering flesh until the last tremors of pleasure had subsided.

When he finally pulled away, I lay there, boneless and sated, my chest rising and falling with each ragged breath. The man straightened, a satisfied smile playing on his lips as he gazed down at me, his chin glistening with the evidence of my arousal.

The applause that followed was a distant sound, a mere echo of the pounding of my heart. As I lay there, fully exposed and utterly spent, I closed my eyes, letting the afterglow wash over me.

My eyes closed, and my legs still spread far apart as I relished the orgasm I had just experienced. The warmth of the release still lingered, pulsating softly through my veins. I was adrift in a sea of satisfaction, the sound of applause a distant echo, when I felt it—a new presence at my entrance.

The man had removed his robe, and now, his hardened cock nudged against my slick, sensitive flesh. There was a moment of hesitation, a silent question hanging in the air, but my body answered before my mind could process the implications. My back arched reflexively, an invitation as old as time.

With a low, guttural sound, he thrust into me. I gasped at the sudden fullness, my eyes snapping open to meet his intense gaze.

He filled me completely, stretching me in a way that felt both foreign and exhilarating.

The room around us seemed to blur, the faces of the onlookers melting into an indistinct tableau. All that mattered was the connection between us, the primal dance of our bodies moving in rhythm.

He set a pace that was both demanding and tender, each stroke stoking the embers of my lingering orgasm into a roaring blaze once more. My fingers clawed at the velvet beneath me, my body writhing beneath the onslaught of pleasure.

I could feel the pressure building again, a tightening in my core that signaled the approach of another release. This one was different, a slow burn that threatened to consume me entirely.

Suddenly, he shifted the angle of his thrusts, hitting a spot deep within me that sent shockwaves of pleasure coursing through my body. My muscles clenched around him, and with a cry that was half pleasure, half surprise, I felt myself hurtling over the edge once more.

The man followed me over the precipice, his own release spilling into me with a final, powerful thrust. He shuddered against me, his body going rigid as he rode out the waves of his climax.

As the man pulled away, I lay there, my body still trembling from the force of our shared climax. The cool air of the room whispered over my damp skin, sending a shiver through me. His essence began to seep from me, trickling down to my buttock.

I was still basking in the afterglow when I felt a new presence between my legs.

My eyes fluttered open, and I found myself looking down at a cascade of golden hair. A blonde woman, her face obscured by a delicate mask, knelt before me. Her hands rested gently on my thighs, parting them further to grant herself better access.

Before I could fully register her intent, her tongue made contact with my sensitive flesh. She lapped at me with a hunger that was both surprising and arousing, her actions sending ripples of pleasure through my over sensitive nerves.

I let out a soft gasp as she delved deeper, her tongue working with practiced precision to collect the mingled evidence of our encounter. Each swipe of her tongue against my swollen flesh sent a jolt of electricity straight to my core, reigniting the embers of my desire.

The room around us faded into obscurity as I became lost in the sensation of her mouth on me. The knowledge that we were in full view of the room's occupants only heightened the intensity of my arousal.

The woman's movements were slow and deliberate, as if she were savoring the taste of our combined essences. The sensation was exquisite, a tender contrast to the fervent claiming that had preceded it.

The blonde woman's ministrations had barely begun to coax my desire back to life when I felt the unmistakable pressure of another presence at my entrance. I barely had time to register the shift in energy before a second man stepped up, his hand wrapped tightly around his hardened cock.

He was tall and muscular, with a ruggedness that hinted at a life lived outdoors. His eyes, a piercing blue, met mine with an intensity that made my breath hitch in my throat. There was no hesitation in his movements as he positioned himself between my legs, the head of his shaft nudging against my wet, willing flesh.

With a single, fluid motion, he thrust into me, filling me with a new fullness that bordered on pain. I let out a sharp cry, my body momentarily overwhelmed by the sudden intrusion. The sound mingled with the low growl of approval that rumbled in his chest as he began to move within me.

His rhythm was relentless, each stroke driving deep and hard, setting off sparks of pleasure-laced pain that radiated throughout my body. I could feel the slickness of our combined arousal as he pistoned in and out, the wet sounds of our coupling echoing lewdly around the room.

The blonde woman hadn't retreated. Instead, she moved to my side, her lips finding mine in a passionate kiss that stole my breath away. Her tongue delved into my mouth, mimicking the thrusts of the man who claimed me so completely, adding another layer of sensation to the maelstrom of ecstasy that threatened to sweep me away.

The man's pace increased, his hips slamming against mine with a force that rocked the pedestal beneath us.

He shuddered against me, his cock pulsing wildly as he emptied himself into my willing body.

As the waves of his orgasm began to ebb, the man slowly withdrew from me, leaving me feeling empty and yearning for more. I lay there, my chest heaving, my body slick with sweat and other, more intimate fluids. The room erupted in applause once more, but I was beyond noticing, lost in the aftermath of my own pleasure.

The man stepped back, a look of satisfaction etched on his face as he surveyed the scene before him—me, sprawled and spent, the blonde woman at my side, her hand now tracing lazy patterns on my overheated skin.

Before I could catch my breath, another figure approached the pedestal. I turned my head, meeting the gaze of yet another stranger who was eager to take his turn with the woman on display. And as he moved into position, his hands already reaching for me, I knew that the night was far from over.

The room had grown even more crowded, the air thick with the scent of sex and the soft murmur of voices blending with the wet sounds of my body being used in every conceivable way. My mind had long since surrendered to the primal rhythm of these nameless encounters, each new partner stoking the fires of my insatiable hunger.

A new figure loomed over me, his eyes dark with lust as they raked over my well-used body. Without a word, he climbed onto the pedestal, his erection bobbing hungrily as he positioned himself between my legs, which were still trembling from the attentions of the last man who had fucked me.

I didn't resist as he entered me, his cock sliding easily into my slick, well-fucked pussy. I was beyond caring about the count, the number of men who had taken their pleasure from me. All that mattered was the feel of this new cock inside me, the way it filled me up, the friction of it moving in and out.

He wasn't gentle, but I didn't want gentle. I wanted to be used, to be nothing more than a vessel for their lust. I wanted to feel the weight of their desire, the urgency of their need as they sought their release within the welcoming depths of my body.

As he fucked me, another man approached, his erection jutting out in front of him. He stood by my head, his fingers twining in my hair as he guided his cock towards my waiting mouth. I opened for him, my tongue darting out to taste the salty pre-cum that beaded at the tip of his shaft.

I moaned around his girth as the man between my legs increased his pace, his thrusts becoming more erratic as he neared his climax. The vibrations from my moans seemed to spur the man in my mouth onward, and he began to fuck my face with the same fervor as his counterpart pounded into my pussy.

The men moved in a synchronized rhythm, their cocks sliding in and out of me in a dance as old as time. I was lost in the sensations, the fullness, the rawness of it all. I could feel the pressure building within me once more, another orgasm threatening to burst forth and shatter what was left of my control.

The man inside me groaned, his body tensing as he reached his peak. I felt the hot flood of his release as he pumped his seed into me, his cock jerking with each pulse of his climax. At the same time, the man in my mouth gave a guttural cry, his fingers tightening in my hair as he too found his release, his cum spurting down my throat.

I swallowed reflexively, my own orgasm crashing over me as I was filled from both ends. Wave after wave of pleasure washed over me, leaving me boneless and sated, at least for the moment.

But as the men withdrew from me, their places quickly taken by others who were eager to claim their turn, I was a willing participant in this carnal parade, a vessel for their desires, and I reveled in every second of it.

As the next man stepped forward, his erection proud and insistent, I opened my arms to him, ready to embrace the next chapter in this endless night of pleasure.

CHAPTER TWENTY-EIGHT

The Breaking Point

D^{*ear diary,*}

I've been staring at this blank page for hours, the ink of my pen hovering just above the paper, as if afraid to commit the truth to writing. But I can't ignore it any longer. I have to face the reality of what I've become, of the person I am when the shadows grow long and the night swallows me whole.

The party. My God, that party was a blur of hands and mouths and bodies, a cacophony of flesh against flesh, and somewhere in the midst of it all, I lost myself. I became a specter, an observer to my own debauchery, watching from a distance as Erika—no, not Erika, but some other woman, some stranger—let herself be consumed by the fire of her own making.

I remember the feel of the cool velvet beneath me, the way they whispered against my skin as I moved, as I was moved by the men who took their turns with me. There was a moment, a single, crystalline moment, when I looked down from above and saw myself, naked and wanton, writhing on that pedestal like some pagan sacrifice to the gods of lust.

The faces of the men melded into one another, a parade of nameless, faceless desires. I couldn't tell you how many there were, nor do I want to know. Each one left a piece of himself inside me, and with every new conquest, I felt myself becoming less, not more. I was a receptacle for their pleasure, my own satisfaction a distant memory, lost in the void of my ever-growing need.

I couldn't feel their touch, not truly. My skin was numb, my senses dulled by the overwhelming tide of bodies that surrounded me—that were part of me, yet completely separate. I was dissociating, my mind retreating into itself as my body was passed from one man to the next like a piece of meat at a feast.

And when the climaxes came—mine and theirs—I felt nothing. No rush of endorphins, no wave of euphoria, just a hollow victory, a fleeting sense of achievement that vanished as quickly as it came. In those moments, I was more machine than woman, a well-oiled apparatus designed for one purpose and one purpose alone: to gratify the carnal appetites of anyone who sought to claim me.

I don't know when it ended or how I found my way back to the solitude of my own home. But here I am, alone with my thoughts and the cold light of day that reveals the truth of my situation. I am out of control. I have let my desires lead me down a path of no return, and I am terrified of what I might become if I continue to walk this road.

I can scarcely bring myself to write these words, to confess the depth of my own self-betrayal. Yesterday, I stood in the shower for what felt like an eternity, the water scalding my skin, trying to wash away the filth that clung to my soul. I told myself that was the end—that the horror of that party would be the wake-up call I so desperately needed. I swore I would not give in to the siren call of my desires, that I would find a way back to the woman I used to be.

But the night came, as it always does, and with it, the hunger that gnaws at my insides, a beast starved for the touch of a stranger's hand. I tried to resist, to ignore the pulsing need that throbbed in time with my heartbeat. I busied myself with the mundane tasks of motherhood and womanhood, trying to drown out the whispers of temptation with the clatter of dishes and the hum of laundry machines.

It didn't work.

I found myself at a bar I'd never visited before, a seedy little dive tucked away in the shadows of the city. The neon sign flickered erratically, casting a sickly glow over the patrons who sought refuge within its walls. I sat alone at the bar, nursing a drink that tasted like regret, watching the people around me with a sense of detachment.

He was nothing special—just another face in the crowd, another body to sate the craving that consumed me. He bought me a drink, and his eyes lingered on my lips as I thanked him. There was something predatory in his gaze, a glint of danger that should have sent me running for the door. But in my reckless pursuit of oblivion, I mistook it for excitement.

We exchanged words, but I can't recall what was said. It didn't matter. The only thing that mattered was the promise of escape that his presence represented. When he suggested we take a walk, I didn't hesitate. I followed him out the back door and into the alley, where the city's underbelly lay exposed beneath the merciless glare of the streetlights.

It happened so fast. One moment, we were kissing, his hands roaming over my body with a roughness that bordered on violence, and the next, he was pushing me against the cold brick wall, wrenching my legs apart with a force that left me gasping for air. He positioned his cock at the entrance of my asshole. I told him to stop, to slow down, but my protests were lost in the darkness that enveloped us.

He didn't listen. He didn't care. My pain was inconsequential, a mere footnote in his pursuit of pleasure. I felt a searing pain as he forced himself into me, a pain that was both physical and emotional, a pain that stripped away the last shreds of my dignity and left me feeling broken and used.

When it was over, he tucked his shirt back into his pants and walked away without a backward glance, leaving me alone in the alley, crying and bleeding and wondering how I had let myself fall so far. I stumbled home in the early hours of the morning, my body aching with a pain that would not soon be forgotten, a stark reminder of the cost of my own self-destruction.

I can't help but wonder: what am I trying to fill with these nameless, faceless encounters? Is it a void within me, a chasm that has opened up over years of feeling neglected and invisible? Or is it something more innate, a hunger that I've always carried with me, dormant until now?

The men, the parties, the thrill of the forbidden—it's like a drug, and I can't deny the rush it gives me. But like any drug, the high doesn't last. It fades, leaving me emptier than before, searching for the next hit, the next fix to make me feel alive, if only for a moment. The pattern is unmistakable, echoing the stories I've heard about addiction, about the way it can consume your life, bit by bit, until there's nothing left but the insatiable need for more.

I see it now, the way my behavior escalates, the way each encounter has to be more intense, more daring than the last to give me the same sense of escape. It's a cycle, a spiral that pulls me deeper into the darkness with every turn. And with each new low, I can hear the faint whisper of a warning bell, the sound of my conscience trying to break through the fog of my desire.

In these rare moments of clarity, I see the life I've built, the faces of my children, Zach and Lily, their smiles wide and trusting, their world still untouched by the shadow that has fallen over mine. I think of Michael, the man I promised to love and honor, the man who, despite his flaws, is the father of my children, the husband who has never lifted a hand against me in anger. What am I doing to them, to the family that means everything to me? How can I risk losing it all for a fleeting moment of pleasure?

The answer is simple: I can't. I won't. I refuse to be a slave to my own desires, to let them dictate my actions and destroy the things that matter most. But admitting that I have a problem is only the first step in a long and arduous journey. I don't know what the future holds, or if I'll ever be free from the grasp of this addiction, but I do know one thing with absolute certainty: I have to try.

I don't know what I'm searching for anymore. Is it validation, excitement, a reprieve from the monotony of my life? Or is it something deeper, some fundamental part of myself that I've lost along the way? All I know is that I'm terrified of what I'm becoming, of the woman whose story I've been documenting in these pages. She's a stranger to me, a shadow that has eclipsed the person I used to be.

For now, this is where my confession ends, but it's also where my journey begins. I won't let this define me. I won't let this be the end of my story. I am more than the sum of my mistakes, and it's time I started acting like it.

For now, I will put down my pen and close this diary, tucking it away in the hidden drawer where my secrets dwell. But tomorrow is a new day, and with it comes the chance for change, for redemption, for the healing that my soul so desperately craves.

I can only hope that I am strong enough to seize it.

CHAPTER TWENTY-NINE

Accidental Discovery

I had sworn to stop, but here I was again. The hotel's bar was upscale enough that I could justify wearing the new red dress that hugged my curves like a second skin. My date for the evening was a hedge fund manager—married, of course—who'd been explicit about what he wanted from our encounter.

I sipped my martini, watching him return from the bathroom, when a familiar silhouette in the lobby froze me mid-swallow. Michael. My husband was walking through the grand entrance, checking his watch.

"Shit," I whispered, nearly dropping my glass. I slid from my barstool and ducked behind a decorative column, mumbling some excuse to my confused date.

My heart hammered against my ribs. What was Michael doing here? He was supposed to be at a client dinner across town. I peered around the column, expecting to see some woman meeting him—perhaps the mysterious Alex I'd found evidence of in the attic.

Instead, a tall man in an impeccably tailored suit approached. They didn't shake hands. The man touched Michael's elbow in a gesture so familiar, so intimate that I felt the floor tilt beneath me. Michael's face transformed—the tight lines around his eyes softened, his smile reaching his eyes in a way I hadn't seen directed at me in years.

"I'll be right back," I murmured to my date, who was growing increasingly annoyed. I moved through the crowd, keeping potted plants and other guests between us as Michael and his companion walked toward the elevators.

They stood closer than business associates would. The stranger leaned in, whispering something that made Michael laugh—a genuine laugh that sent a shock of recognition through me. I knew that laugh. I used to cause that laugh.

When the elevator arrived, I slipped into the adjacent one, jabbing the button for the floor I saw them select. I emerged just in time to see them halfway down the hallway. Before they reached their room, the man glanced around quickly, then pulled Michael toward him. Their lips met in a kiss that was practiced, passionate—the kiss of lovers who had done this many times before.

I pressed myself against the wall, a hand over my mouth to stifle any sound. Michael—my husband—was having an affair with a man.

CHAPTER THIRTY

Parallel Lives

I stumbled back to the elevator, my legs wooden, my mind racing. The hedge fund manager texted twice while I descended to the lobby. I couldn't even remember his name now.

"Something's come up. Family emergency." I texted back, not caring how cliché it sounded.

He replied immediately: "Seriously? After all the buildup?"

I didn't respond, just grabbed my coat from the bar and hurried to my car. My hands shook so badly I dropped my keys twice before managing to unlock the door.

Michael. With a man. The revelation played on loop in my head as I drove home on autopilot. All those late nights. All those business trips. All my resentment at being neglected while I threw myself at strangers.

Our house was dark and quiet. The kids were at friends' houses—a Friday night arrangement that had become convenient for my escapes. I kicked off my heels and moved through the silent rooms, seeing our shared space with new eyes.

In our bedroom, I opened Michael's nightstand drawer—something I hadn't done in months. His iPad sat there, the one he used at home while his work laptop traveled with him. I knew his password—our anniversary date, ironically enough.

The device opened to his messages. I scrolled through, seeing dozens of exchanges with "A.J." The texts were carefully worded but unmistakable in their undertone:

"Can't wait to see you Friday."

"Last night was exactly what I needed."

"Miss your touch already."

I opened his browser history, finding hotel bookings spanning back months. Gay dating apps hidden in folders labeled "Work Resources." Photos buried in his cloud storage—nothing explicit, but intimate nonetheless. Michael and a handsome man with salt-and-pepper hair at dinner. On a hiking trail. Sitting close on a beach at sunset.

A particularly tender message from three days ago read: "Two years since that conference in Chicago. Best mistake I ever made was getting on the wrong elevator and ending up on your floor."

Two years. While I'd been feeling invisible, building resentment, creating my own secret life—Michael had been living his.

I sat on our bed, clutching his iPad, tears streaming down my face. Not tears of anger, but of confusion and recognition. We had both been hiding, both been seeking something we couldn't find at home.

Dear diary,

I've spent three days in a fog. The kids have asked twice if I'm sick. I keep saying I'm just tired, which isn't entirely a lie. I haven't slept more than a few hours since seeing Michael with that man.

It wasn't me. All this time, it wasn't me.

The strange thing is the relief I feel alongside the shock. For years I've been examining my body in mirrors, cataloging every stretch mark, every pound gained, every line around my eyes. I blamed myself for his distance. Too old. Too saggy. Too familiar. Too much a mother and not enough a lover.

But I was fighting a battle that could never be won.

How many times did I initiate only to be rejected? How many nights did I lie awake wondering what was wrong with me? What woman was taking my place in his desire?

There was no woman. There was never going to be a woman.

I laughed until I cried last night, alone in the bathroom with the shower running. The absurdity of it all. Me, building a secret life of meaningless encounters to prove I was still desirable while he built his own parallel existence.

The weight of inadequacy I've carried—it wasn't mine to bear. When he stopped touching me, stopped seeing me, it wasn't because I'd failed as a woman. It was because he couldn't pretend anymore.

I should feel betrayed. I do, in ways. But mostly I feel released from the prison of my own making. The desperate need for validation that drove me to stranger after stranger, risk after risk.

What does it say about our marriage that we both sought comfort elsewhere rather than truth with each other? What does it say about me that my first reaction wasn't anger but recognition?

I don't know what happens next. I don't know if I confront him or wait for him to tell me. I don't know if there's anything left to save or if we've both strayed too far from shore.

But tonight, for the first time in years, I'm not wondering what's wrong with me. And in that space, I can finally breathe.

I canceled three encounters in the days after my discovery. The thought of another anonymous hotel room felt hollow, almost comical in light of what I now knew. But by the fourth day, restlessness crept back in. The habit had grooved itself too deeply into my routine.

This time, though, I approached it differently. I watched Michael leave for his "overnight conference" in Philadelphia, kissing the kids goodbye with practiced ease. I tracked his location on our shared family app, noting when it disappeared—he'd turned it off, as he always did during these trips.

Two hours later, I was checking into the same hotel where his reservation was booked. Not to confront him—something far more perverse. I wanted to observe this shadow life he'd built, to understand the parallel universe that existed alongside our marriage.

From a corner of the lobby bar, I watched Michael arrive. He looked different—lighter, more animated than he ever was at home. When his companion arrived—Alex, I presumed—I studied their interaction with clinical detachment. The subtle touch of hands. The private jokes. The way Michael's eyes never left the other man's face.

I slipped away before they could spot me, heading to my own rendezvous ten blocks away.

"You seem different tonight," my date commented as he poured wine in his downtown apartment.

"Do I?" I smiled, feeling strangely calm. "How so?"

"More present. Less... hurried."

I realized he was right. For the first time, I wasn't rushing toward physical validation, desperately seeking proof of my desirability. I was simply there, choosing this moment rather than fleeing from something else.

Later that week, I tracked another pattern—Michael's Tuesday "late meetings." I followed him to a modest apartment building across town. Waited in my car, watching him emerge two hours later, his face relaxed in a way it never was at home.

Each time I confirmed another piece of his secret life, I felt less frantic in my own pursuits. My encounters became less frequent, more selective. I no longer needed the volume or the risk to feel something.

We were mirrors of each other, Michael and I, both seeking outside what we couldn't ask for at home. Both experts at deception. Both trapped in patterns we'd created to survive.

CHAPTER THIRTY-ONE

Research Phase

I found myself replaying memories of that night with Jen and Mark. The way Jen's touch differed from a man's—softer, more intuitive. How she knew exactly where to linger, when to apply pressure. The electricity between us had been undeniable.

Maybe understanding Michael's attraction to men required experiencing something similar myself. Not the rushed, anonymous encounters I'd been having, but something more... intentional. Something closer to what Michael seemed to have with Alex.

I opened my dating app and adjusted my settings. Women only. I stared at my profile, wondering if I should change my photos, my description. What would appeal to women seeking women? I had no idea. I was navigating unfamiliar territory.

After hesitating, I wrote: "New to this side of myself. Looking for patience and exploration."

Within hours, I had matches. Women with kind eyes and knowing smiles. I studied their profiles carefully, looking for someone who seemed gentle but confident. Someone who could guide me.

I messaged with three before settling on Sophia—an art therapist with warm brown eyes and a profile that mentioned being comfortable with "women on journeys of discovery." Our conversation flowed easily. No crude propositions, no immediate sexual overtones. Instead, we discussed favorite books, travel dreams, and what it meant to discover new aspects of oneself in midlife.

"Would you like to meet for dinner?" she suggested after two days of messaging. "No expectations beyond good food and conversation."

I accepted, feeling nervous in a way I hadn't with men. This wasn't about validation or escape. This was about understanding—both Michael and myself.

As I prepared for our date, I realized I was approaching this differently. I chose an outfit that made me feel comfortable rather than overtly sexy. I applied makeup that enhanced rather than transformed. I wanted to be present, authentic.

What would it be like to connect with a woman the way Michael connected with Alex? Not just physically, but emotionally? I was about to find out.

The restaurant was intimate—soft lighting, tables spaced for privacy. Sophia arrived wearing a simple black dress, her curly hair loose around her shoulders. Her smile was genuine, her handshake lingering just long enough to signal interest without presumption.

"You look lovely," she said, sliding into the seat across from me.

Our conversation flowed naturally—about her work helping people process trauma through art, about my children, about discovering new aspects of ourselves in adulthood. She listened attentively, asked thoughtful questions. I found myself opening up more than I had with anyone in years.

"So what brought you to this exploration?" she asked over dessert, her question gentle but direct.

I hesitated, then decided on honesty. "I recently discovered my husband has been with men. For years, apparently."

Her expression showed compassion without pity. "That must have been shocking."

"The strange thing is... I understand it now in ways I couldn't have before." I traced the rim of my wine glass. "My own... experiences lately have shown me how powerful these desires can be. How they can exist alongside everything else in your life without diminishing it."

Sophia nodded. "Sexuality isn't as fixed as we're taught to believe."

"I've been angry with him for living a double life. But here I am, doing the same thing." I looked down at my hands. "The difference is, I think I understand why now. That hunger for something you can't name until you taste it."

"It's human to seek connection, pleasure, understanding of ourselves," Sophia said. "The deception is what hurts relationships, not the desire itself."

Her words struck me with unexpected force. Michael and I had both been searching, both hiding. Both afraid to speak our truths.

"I've been judging him for exactly what I've been doing," I admitted. "At least he's been consistent in his connection. I've been... scattered. Desperate."

"Maybe you're both just trying to feel whole," Sophia suggested.

I felt something shift inside me—not forgiveness exactly, but recognition. Michael's deception wasn't about rejecting me. It was about embracing a part of himself he couldn't deny, couldn't integrate into our shared life. Just as I'd been doing.

For the first time, I saw our parallel journeys with clarity and without judgment.

Dear diary,

Tonight, I tasted freedom. I didn't just step outside the lines—I danced beyond them with wild abandon. And it was with Sophia, a woman whose name feels like a soft whisper and whose touch is a symphony that played across my skin, awakening parts of me I didn't know were dormant.

We didn't rush. There was no urgency, no race to the finish line. Instead, there was exploration, a mutual uncovering of secrets and desires. Her hands moved with purpose, but also with a tenderness that made my heart ache. She was patient, taking time to learn the curves and contours of my body as if it were a landscape she intended to memorize.

The connection was visceral, soul-deep. It wasn't just the physical act—it was the sharing of a moment that transcended anything I'd ever experienced. With her, I wasn't someone's wife, or someone's mother. I wasn't the sum of my responsibilities, or the keeper of my family's routine. I was just Erika, unbound and unashamed.

Sophia kissed me with a reverence that felt like worship, her lips tracing the outline of my smile, the arch of my clavicle, the swell of my breasts. She listened to the quiet sounds I made, responded to the pressure of my hands, followed the rhythm of my body until we found a cadence that was uniquely ours.

In those hours, I understood Michael's world in a way I never had before. The allure of a connection that society deems forbidden, but nature insists is necessary. The relief of shedding the weight of expectations and just... being.

I saw myself reflected in Sophia's eyes—not just my physical form, but my essence, my spirit. She saw me, all of me, and in that recognition, I felt a jolt of liberation that coursed through my veins like liquid fire.

We were two souls, entwined in a dance as old as time, but somehow entirely new. It was as if I had been living in monochrome, and she had introduced me to a world of color. Every sen-

sation was heightened, every touch ignited a spark that threatened to consume me.

And when we finally lay spent in each other's arms, the world outside our little sanctuary seemed to fade away. There was no guilt, no fear of judgment. Just the steady thrum of our shared heartbeat, and the knowledge that for a single, perfect night, I had been utterly and completely free.

I now see the threads of my own tapestry woven with new colors—ones that are bold and vibrant, and unapologetically mine. I understand Michael's hidden life with a compassion I didn't possess before. We've both been seeking the same thing—authenticity, acceptance, and the courage to live our truths.

As I close my eyes, the warmth of Sophia's memory wraps around me like a lover's embrace. I am changed. I am alive. And though the future is uncertain, I am ready to face it with the lessons of this night etched into my soul.

CHAPTER THIRTY-TWO

The Almost Confession

The familiar sound of Michael's key in the door pulled me from my thoughts. Footsteps in the hallway, the rustle of a paper bag, and his voice calling out with unusual warmth.

"Erika? You home?"

"In the kitchen," I answered, closing my laptop where I'd been updating my private calendar.

He appeared in the doorway holding a bottle of wine and a small bouquet of tulips—my favorites, not roses. The gesture was so unexpected I almost laughed.

"What's the occasion?" I asked, accepting both with careful hands.

"Do I need one?" His smile seemed forced, eyes not quite meeting mine. "I thought maybe we could have dinner, just us. Kids are both out tonight, right?"

I nodded, studying him. The slight tremor in his hands as he uncorked the wine. The way he'd dressed in the blue shirt I'd once told him brought out his eyes. The nervous energy radiating from him as he moved around our kitchen with uncharacteristic attention to detail.

"I made reservations, but then canceled them," he admitted, pulling ingredients from the refrigerator. "Thought it might be better to talk here. Private."

Talk. The word hung between us, loaded with unspoken meaning.

"I can help," I offered, moving beside him at the counter.

Our hands brushed as I reached for a knife. He didn't pull away. Instead, he paused, fingers lingering against mine.

"Erika, I—" He stopped, swallowed hard. "There's something I've been wanting to—needing to tell you."

The cutting board between us suddenly seemed like an ocean. I recognized the look on his face—I'd seen it in my mirror countless times. The desperate need to confess warring with the terror of consequences.

"Michael," I said softly, "whatever it is—"

"No, please. Let me get through this." He poured wine with shaking hands, spilling a few drops on the counter. "I've rehearsed this so many times, but now that I'm here..."

I waited, heart pounding. For the first time in years, I truly saw him—not the husband who had rejected me, but a man trapped in his own silence, carrying a weight I understood all too well.

"We should sit," he suggested, gesturing toward the living room. "This isn't a standing conversation."

The living room felt miles away. Each step we took toward the couch stretched like a lifetime of missed connections between us. Michael's shoulders hunched forward as if physically carrying his confession. I clutched my wine glass like a shield.

"Mom? Dad?" Lily's voice shattered the moment, followed by the front door slamming. Her footsteps thundered through the entryway, each one erasing the fragile bridge we'd begun to build.

Michael froze, his face a portrait of interrupted courage. The words he'd gathered scattered like startled birds.

Our daughter appeared in the doorway, mascara streaked down her cheeks, hair disheveled. Her red-rimmed eyes darted between us, registering the wine, the flowers, the unusual tableau of her parents about to have an actual conversation.

"What's wrong, honey?" I set my glass down, maternal instinct overriding everything else.

"Jill and everyone—they—" Her voice cracked as fresh tears spilled. "They posted these awful things about me in the group chat, and then Madison's mom called and said I can't come to the lake house this weekend because of something I supposedly said, which I never did, and now everyone's blocked me and—"

Michael's confession evaporated into the air between us, replaced by the immediate crisis of teenage social warfare. His face cycled through emotions—disappointment, relief, resignation—before settling into concerned father mode.

"Slow down, Lil," he said, placing his untouched wine on the counter. "Start from the beginning."

As Lily collapsed into tears against my shoulder, I caught Michael's eye over her head. Something important had slipped away from us. The courage he'd mustered might not return so easily.

He gave me a small, sad smile that said everything: Not now. Not yet. Maybe never.

I nodded slightly, understanding completely. Our moment had passed, swept away by the current of family life that had both sustained and separated us for years.

"I'll make some tea," he murmured, turning back toward the kitchen, the weight still visibly heavy on his shoulders.

The flowers sat forgotten on the counter, their brief promise of reconciliation already wilting.

Dear diary,

It's always so hard starting a new blank page. The pen trembles in my hand, like it knows the weight of what I'm about to write.

Michael almost told me tonight. I saw it in his eyes—that same desperate need for confession I've felt crawling under my own skin for months. The wine, the flowers, the carefully chosen shirt. He'd planned it all, summoned his courage, and then Lily burst in with her teenage catastrophe.

Should I confront him? The evidence is there—the mysterious Alex, the business trips that weren't business, the browser history, and now that almost-confession. I could lay it all out, force his hand. "I know about him, Michael. I know you're gay or bi or whatever label fits. I know you've been living a lie."

But wouldn't that make me the biggest hypocrite alive? Me, with my spreadsheets of strangers and secret credit card and afternoon "client meetings" that leave me sore and empty?

If I confront him, don't I have to confess too? And if we both confess, what's left of us? Two people who've been lying to each other, cheating on each other, for God only who knows how long.

Maybe I should wait. Let him find his courage again. He was so close tonight—I saw the words forming, saw fifteen years of marriage balanced on the edge of his tongue.

But what if he never tells me? What if we keep circling each other in this house, both carrying secrets that are slowly poisoning us?

The doctor called today. The antibiotics are working. The infection isn't serious, she said. This time. Her eyes said what her professional ethics wouldn't allow: Be more careful or next time it could be worse.

I'm running out of time. My body is sending warnings I can't ignore. Michael's eyes tonight were sending messages I can't unsee.

Wait or confront? Let him speak first or force his hand?

God, I don't know what's right anymore. I just know we can't keep living like this. Something has to break.

Maybe it's already broken.

CHAPTER THIRTY-THREE

Rehearsing Truth

The speedometer crept past seventy as I merged onto the highway. Another Friday, another fabricated client meeting, another hotel room with a stranger waiting. I barely registered the drive anymore—muscle memory guiding me while my mind churned elsewhere.

"I know about Alex." No, too accusatory. "Michael, I think we need to talk about what's happening with us." Better, but still loaded.

I rehearsed the confrontation for the hundredth time, testing different tones like trying on clothes. Angry wife? Understanding partner? Wounded victim?

The bitter irony wasn't lost on me. Here I was, driving to meet man number—God, I'd lost count—feeling somehow betrayed that my husband desired men. The hypocrisy made me laugh out loud in the empty car, a harsh sound that surprised even me.

What right did I have to feel deceived? While he kissed a man in a hotel elevator, I was upstairs with my legs wrapped around a stranger whose last name I never bothered to learn.

If I confronted him with anger, wouldn't I be forcing him to confront me the same way? If I approached with understanding, could I reasonably expect the same grace in return?

I imagined the conversation unfolding in different ways. In one version, we screamed and threw things, fifteen years shattered like wine glasses against walls. In another, we cried together, broken but somehow relieved. In the darkest version, cold silence, followed by lawyers.

The exit for the hotel approached. I flipped my turn signal, then canceled it, then flipped it again.

"I've been sleeping with other men." The words felt strange in my mouth, even practiced alone. "It started because I felt invisible to you. I felt like a ghost in our marriage."

Would he understand that? Could he? Or would he only see betrayal, not the desperate search for connection underneath?

Maybe we were both seeking what the other couldn't provide. Maybe we'd both been drowning in the same house, neither able to throw the other a lifeline.

Would confession save us or destroy us? Would honesty create space for something new or burn everything to ash?

I pulled into the hotel parking lot, cut the engine, and sat. My phone buzzed—probably him, wondering if I was still coming.

One part of me wanted to start the car again, drive home, wait for Michael in the kitchen, and finally have the conversation we'd been avoiding.

Instead, I grabbed my purse and stepped out into the cool air. One last time, I told myself. One final escape before reality.

CHAPTER THIRTY-FOUR

Rock Bottom

T he hotel room door clicked shut behind me, sealing off the world I knew. The man—Marcus, Mark, something with an 'M'—stood by the window, silhouetted against the city lights. He was handsome enough, in that anonymous, hotel-bar sort of way.

We exchanged the usual pleasantries, our voices overlaid with a practiced nonchalance. But as we moved to the bed, something felt off. My body went through the motions, but my mind was miles away, tangled in thoughts of Michael.

Michael, whose kisses I'd once craved like water. Michael, whose secrets I'd unwittingly mirrored.

I closed my eyes as 'M' touched me, trying to lose myself in the sensation. But each caress felt like an echo of something I'd already lost. I was searching for a spark that refused to ignite, a connection that eluded me even as our bodies entwined.

When it was over, we lay side by side, a chasm between us on the king-sized bed. He was already reaching for his phone, scrolling through messages, the post-coital glow replaced by the blue light of screens.

I excused myself to the bathroom, splashing water on my face, looking into eyes that seemed to belong to someone else. The woman in the mirror was a stranger—a ghost who haunted hotel rooms and bar stools, chasing a feeling she couldn't quite capture.

I was still in the bathroom when his phone rang. Through the partially closed door, I heard 'M' answer with a casual "Hey babe."

My stomach twisted. I'd never asked if he was married. Never wanted to know.

"Just finishing up with the client... Yeah, dinner with Johnson went long."

I gripped the edge of the sink. The lies sounded so practiced, so smooth—just like mine.

"Of course I miss you too... No, I'll be home tomorrow... Kiss the kids for me."

Kids. He had children waiting for him. Children who thought their dad was at a business dinner. Just like Zach and Lily thought I was at a bookkeeping conference last month.

I stared at my reflection, seeing for the first time the web I'd spun around my life—around all our lives. How many other spouses had I helped deceive? How many families had I unwittingly touched with my selfishness?

When I emerged, 'M' was already buttoning his shirt, his wedding band back on his finger.

"Sorry about that. Wife checking in." He smiled, no trace of guilt in his expression. "You know how it is."

But I did know. I knew exactly how it was—the careful accounting of time, the deleted texts, the rehearsed excuses. I'd become an expert in deception.

"Everything okay?" he asked, noticing my silence.

"What happens when they find out?" The question escaped before I could stop it.

He laughed. "They don't find out. That's the point."

"But what if they do?" I pressed, suddenly needing to know. "What happens then?"

I wrapped the sheet tighter around myself. "I'm just... confused. And sad, I guess. Why do you do it? What are you missing at home?"

His hands paused on his belt buckle. For a moment, I thought he'd dismiss the question with another practiced line, but something in my expression must have reached him.

"Why do I do it?" He sank onto the edge of the bed. "That's a heavy question for what this is supposed to be."

He ran a hand through his hair, suddenly looking older in the dim light.

"Nothing dramatic. No tragic story." He shrugged. "My wife's great. Kids are great. Life's... fine."

"Fine," I echoed.

"Yeah. Fine. Predictable. Safe." He stared at his hands. "Sometimes I just want to feel something different. To be someone else for a few hours."

The words hit me like a physical blow. How many times had I thought the exact same thing?

"And you?" he asked, turning the question back on me. "What are you missing?"

I opened my mouth to answer, but found I couldn't form the words. What was I missing? Passion? Attention? Or was it something deeper—something I couldn't find in hotel rooms with strangers?

"I don't even know anymore," I whispered, the truth of it settling over me like a heavy blanket. "I thought I knew when this started. I thought I was just... invisible at home. Undesired."

"And now?"

"Now I think maybe I was running from something instead of toward it." I blinked back unexpected tears. "Maybe we both are."

He nodded slowly, a flash of recognition crossing his face. For the first time since entering the room, we truly saw each other—not as bodies to be used, but as people carrying the same hollow ache.

"Does it help?" I asked. "All of this—does it fill whatever's missing?"

"For a moment," he said softly. "Just for a moment. Then it's gone, and I need more."

Like an addiction. The realization settled in my chest with crushing clarity.

His face hardened. "Look, I didn't come here for this kind of talk."

As he gathered his things, I saw myself reflected in his actions—the compartmentalization, the casual dismissal of consequences. Was this what I'd become? Was this what Michael had become too?

We were living parallel lives of secrets, Michael and I. Both of us searching outside our marriage for something we couldn't name, both of us hiding, lying, pretending. The secrets weren't just hurting our marriage—they were destroying us individually, turning us into people I barely recognized.

The hotel room door closed behind him with a soft click, leaving me alone with the rumpled sheets and the weight of realization.

I sank onto the edge of the bed, my hands shaking as I reached for my purse. Inside was the small notebook I'd started carrying—not my full diary, but a place to jot thoughts between encounters. I flipped it open, scanning entries from the past few months. The progression was stark: from excited descriptions of feeling desired to clinical accounts of positions and places, ending with today's hollow emptiness.

My phone buzzed with a text from Michael: "Working late. Don't wait up."

I stared at those now familiar words, imagining him typing them—perhaps sitting beside his own secret, his own "M." The lie was so familiar, so routine, that neither of us questioned it anymore. We'd built parallel lives of deception, each secret taking us further from who we used to be.

These secrets weren't just destroying our marriage—they were destroying us individually. The woman I'd become wasn't someone I recognized or respected. Each encounter left me feeling more fragmented, more disconnected from myself. And Michael—was he experiencing the same slow erosion of self? The same gradual replacement of intimacy with empty physical connection?

I thought of Lily asking if things were okay between her parents. Children always know. They sense the fault lines in a home long before the earthquake hits.

I closed the notebook and walked to the hotel window, looking out at the city lights. Each pinprick of brightness represented a home, a life, a truth I'd been running from. The secret life I'd built wasn't freedom—it was another kind of prison. One I'd constructed myself, brick by brick, lie by lie.

And Michael was trapped in his own version of the same prison. Whatever he was seeking in the arms of other men, it clearly wasn't filling the void either. We were both lost, searching for something we couldn't name, destroying ourselves in the process.

The truth would hurt—god, it would hurt like hell—but these secrets were killing us slowly. Something had to change.

CHAPTER THIRTY-FIVE

The Confrontation

I waited until the house fell silent. Zach and Lily were at sleepovers—Zach at his basketball teammate's house, Lily at her first "high school" party, hosted by a sophomore girl whose parents I'd carefully vetted. The timing felt deliberate, cosmic even, though I'd planned it meticulously.

Michael sat in his home office, the blue light of his laptop illuminating his face. I watched him from the doorway, this man I'd shared a life with for fifteen years. This stranger.

"We need to talk." My voice sounded steadier than I felt, belying the earthquake inside me. My hands trembled slightly, so I crossed my arms to hide it.

He looked up, that familiar crease between his eyebrows deepening like a fault line. The blue screen reflected in his reading glasses as he frowned. "Can it wait? I've got this proposal due tomorrow morning, and I'm barely halfway through the financials—"

"No, it can't." I placed the business card on his desk. Alex Jenkins. The handwritten number scrawled in blue ink. "I found this. And the movie tickets from your 'business trip' to Chicago." The evidence felt absurdly small against the weight of what they represented. Two flimsy pieces of paper that somehow contained the collapse of our marriage, our history, our future—all of it reduced to these damning scraps.

His face drained of color, as if someone had pulled a plug. The confident man who'd been absorbed in spreadsheets seconds ago vanished, replaced by someone caught, cornered. His fingers hovered over the keyboard, frozen mid-sentence like his thoughts. "Erika, I can explain—" His voice cracked on my name, the sound of it like a plea already forming.

"I saw you, Michael. At the Marriott downtown. With a man." The words hung in the air between us, irrevocable. Each syllable felt like a stone dropping into still water, sending ripples across the careful surface of our marriage.

He stared at the card, his fingers trembling slightly against the polished wood of his desk. A muscle twitched in his jaw as he struggled to maintain composure, his eyes refusing to meet mine. "It's not what you think." His voice was hollow, unconvincing even to his own ears, the default response of someone caught in a truth they weren't prepared to face.

"Don't." The word came out sharper than intended, a blade unsheathed. "Please don't lie to me anymore." My voice cracked slightly on the last word, betraying the fragile control I was desperately maintaining.

The silence stretched between us, years of unspoken truths hanging in the balance, thick enough to choke on. The gentle ticking of his office clock marked the seconds, each one pulling us further into a reality neither of us had been ready to acknowledge. His wedding band caught the light as his hand tensed against the desk, a golden reminder of promises that now seemed built on sand.

"How long have you known?" he finally asked, his voice barely audible, like a confession.

"Not long enough. Not nearly as long as you've been living this double life." I could taste the bitterness coating each syllable.

Michael pushed away from the desk, pacing the small office like a caged animal. "It's not—" He stopped, pressed his palms against his eyes as if trying to push the truth back inside. "It's complicated."

"Then uncomplicate it for me." My heart hammered against my ribs, dreading and demanding answers in equal measure.

He collapsed back into his chair, defeated, shoulders caving inward. "I'm bisexual." The words seemed to physically pain him, dragged from somewhere deep. "But men have always be en... it's always been stronger with men."

I leaned against the doorframe for support, feeling the solid wood against my shoulder blades, needing something—anything—to anchor me. "Then why marry me? Why this whole life?"

His eyes met mine, filled with a different kind of pain than I'd expected. Not the guilt of being caught, but something deeper, more fundamental, almost primal.

"Because I loved you, Erika. I still do." His voice broke, splintering like glass. "I wanted this life—you, the kids, all of it. I wanted to be normal."

"Normal," I repeated, the word bitter on my tongue, poisonous.

"That's not—" He shook his head, frustration creasing his features. "I wanted to be the person everyone expected me to be. The person I thought I should be." His words carried the weight of a lifetime of compromise and self-denial.

CHAPTER THIRTY-SIX

Cards on the Table

Michael's hands shook as he clasped them together, knuckles turning white with pressure. His voice emerged as a broken whisper, stripped of all pretense.

"Do you want a divorce?" The question hung between us, fragile and devastating. Tears welled in his eyes, one breaking free to trace a path down his cheek. He didn't brush it away, just let it fall as if he no longer had the right to comfort even himself. "I'd understand if you do."

The word 'divorce' echoed in the small office, bouncing off the walls of our fifteen years together. It was the first time either of us had spoken it aloud, though I'd turned it over in my mind countless times during my own secret explorations.

I watched him crumble before me, this man I'd built a life with, shared children with, the man whose touch I'd once craved and whose absence had driven me to seek validation in the arms of strangers. His vulnerability was raw, exposed like a nerve.

"I don't know what I want," I admitted, the truth of it surprising even me. Despite all my mental rehearsals over and over in my mind, despite the righteous anger I'd nursed, I found myself unmoored in the face of his pain. "I thought I did, but now..."

His shoulders slumped further, the perfect posture he always maintained—another mask, I now realized—completely abandoned. More tears followed the first, and his breath hitched with the effort of containing a sob.

"I never meant to hurt you," he whispered. "I tried so hard to be who I thought I needed to be. Who everyone wanted me to be."

"And I wasn't enough," I said, the words escaping before I could stop them.

Michael looked up sharply, eyes wide. "No, Erika, that's not—" He struggled to find the words. "It was never about you not being enough. It was about me not being honest. With you. With myself."

The irony wasn't lost on me. How could I condemn his dishonesty when my own secrets weighed so heavily? When my body still carried the evidence of my own double life?

I looked at my husband, this stranger I'd shared a bed with for fifteen years, and felt something unexpected—kinship in our mutual deception.

"I have something to tell you too." My voice sounded distant, like it belonged to someone else. The rehearsed speeches I'd practiced in my car evaporated, leaving only raw truth. "I've been unfaithful."

Michael's face registered confusion, then disbelief. "What?"

"Not just once." The words tumbled out now, unstoppable. "Many times. With many men."

His body went completely still. "What are you talking about?"

"I've been sleeping with other people. Strangers, mostly." I wrapped my arms around myself, suddenly cold despite the warmth of the room. "It started after my birthday. When you forgot. Again."

Michael's mouth opened, closed, opened again. "Erika—"

"I felt invisible," I continued, unable to stop now that I'd begun. "Like I was disappearing. You wouldn't look at me, wouldn't touch me. I thought it was me. That I wasn't attractive anymore."

His eyes widened in horror. "That was never—"

"So I found people who would see me. Who made me feel desired." The shame I'd expected to overwhelm me transformed into something else—a terrible clarity. "It became... addictive. The attention. The risk. The feeling of being wanted."

Michael sank back into his chair, face ashen. "How many?"

I shook my head. "I don't know. I stopped counting." The admission hung between us, brutal in its honesty. "I have a spreadsheet."

A bitter laugh escaped him, tinged with hysteria. "A spreadsheet."

"I know how that sounds."

"Do you?" His voice cracked. "Because I don't think you do."

"I was filling a void," I said, the words sounding hollow even to my own ears. "But it just got bigger. Emptier. Nothing was enough."

Michael stared at me as if seeing me for the first time. "While I was hiding who I was, you were—"

"Becoming someone I don't recognize," I finished for him. "Someone I'm not sure I like very much."

The silence stretched between us, thick and suffocating. Michael stared at the family photo on the bookshelf—the four of us at the beach last summer, all perfect smiles hiding perfect lies. I studied my hands, noticing how tightly I'd been gripping my wedding ring, turning it around and around on my finger.

Minutes passed. The tick of the clock on the wall marked time in a house that suddenly felt like it belonged to strangers.

"So," Michael finally said, his voice hoarse. "While I was sneaking off to meet Alex..."

"I was meeting men from dating apps," I finished.

"And all this time..."

"We were both living double lives."

"Under the same roof."

"Sleeping in the same bed."

"Both feeling—"

"Guilty and relieved at the same time," I said.

Michael's eyes met mine, something shifting in them. "Relieved?"

"That I had a reason to be out of the house when you wanted to be."

His mouth twitched. "I used to be grateful when you'd schedule those bookkeeping conferences."

"There were no conferences."

"I know that now."

I felt a bubble of something unexpected rise in my chest. "And there were no late meetings with clients from Singapore."

"No," he admitted. "There weren't."

"We've been covering for each other without even knowing it."

The absurdity of it hit me all at once—the elaborate lies, the careful scheduling, the two of us tiptoeing around each other's deceptions, unwittingly creating the perfect environment for the other's infidelity.

A sound escaped me—not quite a laugh, not quite a sob.

Michael looked startled, then his shoulders began to shake. A snort escaped him, then another.

"We've been—" he tried, but couldn't finish.

"I know," I gasped, the laughter building now, unstoppable.

"All this time—" he managed before dissolving again.

We were both laughing now, genuine laughter I hadn't heard from either of us in years. Tears streamed down my face, and I couldn't tell if they were from humor or grief or both.

"We're a disaster," I choked out between fits of laughter.

"The perfect disaster," Michael agreed, wiping his eyes. "Perfectly synchronized in our complete dysfunction."

The laughter faded, leaving us in a strange calm—like the eerie stillness after a storm. Michael's face grew serious again, his eyes finding mine across the room.

"What do you want, Erika?" he asked, his voice stripped of pretense. "Not what you think you should want. What do you actually want?"

The question caught me off guard. For months, I'd been chasing sensation, not stopping to examine the root of my hunger.

"I want to feel alive," I said finally. "To be seen. Not as a mother or a wife or someone's fantasy, but as me." My throat tightened. "I want to matter to someone."

Michael nodded slowly. "I've never felt seen either. Not really." He ran a hand through his hair. "With men, I could be... parts of myself I couldn't show anyone else. Not even you."

"Why couldn't you show me?"

"Because I was terrified," he admitted. "Of losing everything. Of you looking at me differently."

"I've looked at myself differently for years," I said. "Like I was slowly disappearing."

Michael's expression shifted to something like recognition. "I felt the same way. Like I was fading out, piece by piece."

"So we both went looking for ourselves in other people."

"And did you find what you needed?" he asked.

I considered the question, really considered it. "No," I said finally. "I found distraction. Validation. Sometimes pleasure. But afterward, I always felt emptier."

"Me too," he whispered. "It was like chasing a high that never quite satisfied."

"What do you want, Michael?"

He closed his eyes briefly. "I want to stop hiding. To stop performing." When he looked at me again, his gaze was clear. "I want someone who knows all of me and stays anyway."

"I don't know if I can be that person anymore," I admitted. "I don't know if you can be that for me either."

"Maybe we've both been looking for something the other can't give."

"Or maybe," I said carefully, "we never really asked each other to try."

CHAPTER THIRTY-SEVEN

The Negotiation

The silence that followed felt different from before—less suffocating, more contemplative. The weight between us had shifted somehow, like storm clouds parting just enough to let in a sliver of clarity.

"We've been married fifteen years," Michael said finally, his voice soft but steady. "That's a lot to throw away. Fifteen years of memories. Vacations. Family holidays. The life we built."

"Is it, though? If we've both been looking elsewhere?" I traced the rim of my coffee mug, watching the ripples form. "Maybe what we've been holding onto is just the idea of us, not what we actually became."

He considered this, running a hand through his salt-and-pepper hair—when had it gotten so gray? His eyes, when they met mine, held something I hadn't seen in months. Determination, perhaps.

"Maybe what we need isn't to end the marriage, but to reimagine it. To build something new from the foundation we already have."

I raised an eyebrow, skepticism and curiosity mingling in equal measure. "What does that mean? Exactly what kind of arrangement are you suggesting here?"

"What if..." he hesitated, choosing his words carefully, fingers tracing the rim of his own mug. "What if we stopped expecting each other to be everything? What if we acknowledged that we both have needs the other can't fulfill? We've been trying to fit into roles that maybe we've outgrown."

"You mean an open marriage?" The words felt strange in my mouth, yet somehow less shocking than they would have been months ago. A year ago, I might have thrown my coffee at him. Now, I was turning the concept over like a curious artifact.

"Maybe. Or something uniquely ours." His voice softened as he leaned forward, elbows on his knees. "I don't have a blueprint. I just know I'm not ready to lose us completely, even if what we become looks different than what we started as."

I thought about the men I'd been with—the rush that came not just from the sex itself, but from the secrecy, the forbidden nature of it all. "I think part of what drove me was the thrill of breaking rules," I admitted. "Once I started, it became almost... addictive." The confession hung between us, raw and unvarnished. There was something liberating about finally speaking this truth aloud, acknowledging the dark current that had carried me along. Each encounter had offered not just physical release, but a momentary escape from the person I was supposed to be, the boundaries I'd always respected until they began to feel like prison walls.

"I understand that," Michael nodded, his face softening with recognition. "For me, the shame was paralyzing. I couldn't even consider talking to you about it. I thought you'd leave me immediately if you knew. The fear of losing you was worse than living with the guilt."

"Instead I was doing the same thing," I said with a bitter laugh that held no humor. "Both of us trapped in identical cages of our own making."

We both fell quiet, processing the painful irony. The silence between us felt different now—less like a wall and more like a shared space where our separate confessions hung suspended, mingling together in the still air around us.

"What if..." Michael started, then stopped, a flush creeping up his neck. His fingers twitched nervously against his thigh before he found his courage again. "What if we experienced some of this together?"

"Together?" My pulse quickened, the word hanging between us with new and dangerous potential. I could feel heat rising to my own face, mirroring his.

"We both enjoy being with men," he said carefully, his eyes searching mine for any sign of rejection or disgust. "What if, instead of sneaking around separately, we shared that? Found a way to explore this side of ourselves without the secrecy that's been tearing us apart."

The image flashed in my mind—Michael and I with another man, all boundaries dissolved, nothing hidden between us anymore. A shiver ran through me that had nothing to do with fear and everything to do with unexpected desire.

"That would be..." I searched for the right word, my mouth suddenly dry as the possibilities unfurled before me.

"Honest," he supplied, his voice dropping to a husky whisper. "Finally honest with each other after all this time."

"I think it would be incredibly arousing," I admitted, surprised by my own boldness. "Watching you. Being watched by you. Sharing something we've both kept separate for so long."

His eyes darkened, pupils dilating as he leaned slightly closer. "Sharing that level of intimacy, after all this deception... it could heal something between us that I thought was broken beyond repair."

"But the kids can never know," I said firmly, drawing a clear boundary around this fragile new understanding. "This stays completely private from them. They've been through enough already."

"Absolutely," he agreed immediately, nodding with conviction. "This is just between us—and whoever we invite in. The children deserve stability, not confusion about what we're exploring."

"We do love each other," I said, realizing as I spoke that it was true. The revelation settled over me with surprising comfort. Despite everything—the fights, the distance, the betrayals—there was still something there—history, family, understanding. A foundation we'd built over years that couldn't simply vanish.

"We do," he echoed, a hint of wonder in his voice. "Maybe not in the way we thought we should, or the way everyone told us love is supposed to look, but in our own way. Something real, if unconventional."

———————◀O▶———————

Dear diary,

For the first time in years, I feel like I'm seeing Michael—really seeing him. Not the husband I thought I married, but the complex, conflicted man he actually is. And strangely, I feel more connected to him now than when I believed our lies. The thought of experiencing pleasure together, of sharing that vulnerability instead of hiding it... I'm nervous, but also more excited than I've been in years. Maybe this is what intimacy really is—not the fairy tale, but the messy truth of who we really are. There's something liberating about dropping the pretense, about acknowledging our flaws and desires without judgment. When he looked at me tonight, there was recognition in his eyes—like he was finally seeing me too. All those years wasted on perfect performances when what we both needed was simply to be known. Tomorrow feels like the first day of something new, something real. I'm terrified, of course. Real intimacy means real risk. But for once, the possibility of genuine connection seems worth whatever pain might come with it.

CHAPTER THIRTY-EIGHT

Boundaries and Rules

The next morning, they sat at the kitchen table with fresh coffee, notepads, and a shared sense of purpose. The kids were at school. No interruptions. No hiding.

"We need rules," Erika said, pen poised above paper. "Clear boundaries we both agree to."

Michael nodded. "Complete honesty. That's non-negotiable."

"About everything?" Erika's voice caught. "Even the past?"

"Especially the past. I've spent too many years hiding." Michael reached for her hand. "But I don't need a detailed spreadsheet of your encounters."

Erika's cheeks burned. She'd deleted the spreadsheet last night.

"We should both get tested," she said quietly. "I haven't always been... careful."

"I have been, but yes. That's essential." Michael wrote it down. "And protection always, with everyone."

"Including each other?"

Michael looked up. "Until we're both cleared, yes. After that...No way!"

They continued methodically: no mutual friends or colleagues; no overnight absences without explanation to the other; veto power over any potential partner; regular check-ins about feelings.

"What about the kids?" Erika asked.

"Our sex life was never their business before, and it still isn't now," Michael said firmly. "This is between us, as adults."

"But if they suspect something..."

"We're still their parents. We still love each other. That hasn't changed."

Erika nodded. "And the apps? I should delete mine."

"Me too. Too impersonal. Too risky." Michael reached for his phone, opened his hidden folder. "Let's do it together."

They deleted accounts, uninstalled apps, purged messages. With each deletion, Erika felt lighter.

"We rebuild from here," Michael said. "With intention, not desperation."

"What if one of us falls in love with someone else?"

Michael considered this. "Then we talk about it honestly. That's the point—no more secrets. You said you'd been with so many men you'd lost count. Out of all those men, how many did you fall in love with?"

"Good point, None. I get it. Love takes more than just sex. I want this to make us stronger," Erika said. "Not tear us apart."

"It already has." Michael squeezed her hand. "Yesterday we were strangers living in the same house. Today we're actually seeing each other."

Erika felt tears forming. "I'm scared."

"Me too. But I'm not alone anymore." Michael's voice broke slightly. "And neither are you."

———◆○◆———

They sat together on the couch that evening, laptop balanced between them. The kids were in their rooms, doors closed, headphones on, lost in their own digital worlds. The house was quiet except for the occasional muffled thump of bass from their son's room.

"So," Erika said, fidgeting with the hem of her shirt, her fingers nervously pleating the fabric. "How are we going to find people to uhm..."

"To play with?" Michael finished, a small smile playing at his lips. His eyes crinkled at the corners, that familiar expression that still made her heart skip after all these years.

They both chuckled, the tension breaking slightly. The nervous energy between them felt both strange and exciting, like teenagers planning something forbidden.

"Yes," Erika confirmed, meeting his eyes. She took a deep breath, steadying herself.

Michael turned toward the screen, the blue light illuminating his face. "I'm thinking we use a swingers dating site, but we choose together. A man, a woman, a couple, hopefully the guy is bi. But we do it together and we agree on them together." His finger hovered over the trackpad, waiting for her nod of approval before clicking further into this new territory.

"I like that idea." Erika nodded, then hesitated, tucking a strand of hair behind her ear. "I have to ask though. What about us going off separately without the other? Is that something you'd be comfortable with at some point?"

Michael considered this for a moment, his expression thoughtful as he leaned back in his chair.

"I think we should go on a case by case basis. But again this is about complete honesty. No sneaking off. If either of us want a solo encounter, the other has to agree to it." He reached for her hand, giving it a gentle squeeze. "Trust is everything here. We need to communicate about everything, especially the uncomfortable parts."

Erika twisted her wedding ring, gathering courage. The cool metal band slid against her skin as she summoned the resolve to broach a topic that had been lingering in her mind.

"I need to ask another question. This one may be a bit more uncomfortable." Her voice was steady, but her fingers continued their nervous fidgeting.

"What is it Erika?" Michael's expression grew serious, the earlier lightness in his features giving way to something more guarded. He leaned forward slightly, his shoulders tensing.

"What about... Alex?" She watched his face carefully, noting every subtle change in his expression. Her gaze remained unflinching as she pressed on. "It sure looked to me like that relationship was more than just casual fucking. You two seemed to be involved for quite awhile." The words hung in the air between them, heavy with unspoken implications and the weight of past entanglements.

Michael sighed deeply, closing the laptop with a quiet snap. His shoulders sagged slightly as he ran a hand through his hair.

"Yeah, I've been struggling with that as well," he admitted, his voice low and tinged with resignation. "Erika, I love you—I truly do—and it's true I do have deep feelings for Alex. We've been seeing each other for a long time, almost two years now, but I will give it up." His eyes met hers, searching for understanding. "I want us to work. I need us to work. He'll just have to understand." Michael's mouth tightened into a thin line before he added, "He has a wife at home as well. This was always going to be complicated."

Erika reached for his hand, her fingers entwining with his. "I love you too much to make you give him up. I don't know how or why but I somehow understand those feelings. They're part of who you are."

"Thank you, that's why I love you so much." Michael's voice was thick with emotion, his eyes glistening slightly. "I never thought you'd be so understanding."

"Maybe you could introduce me to him sometime. I'd love to know the man I share my husband with." Her lips curved upward into a mischievous smile. "Hell, maybe we could all enjoy a little fun together. Maybe he could be one of our primary playmates," she said, chuckling softly, a hint of genuine curiosity in her tone.

Michael's eyes widened, a flush creeping up his neck. "I feel pretty sure he would be into that. He has hated all the secrecy as much as I have." He hesitated for a moment, then reopened the laptop, the screen casting a soft glow across his face. "Now let's check out some swinger sites and see if we can find anyone that tickles our fancy, shall we? This could be the beginning of something amazing for us."

CHAPTER THIRTY-NINE

The Shared Experience

The boutique hotel lobby gleamed with polished marble and understated elegance. Erika shifted her overnight bag to her other shoulder, hyper aware of Michael's presence beside her. Their arms brushed as he stepped forward to the reception desk.

"Reservation for Lawrence," Michael said, his voice carrying a hint of nervous tension that only Erika would recognize.

The receptionist tapped at her keyboard, manicured nails clicking against the keys. "Yes, Mr. and Mrs. Lawrence. King suite for one night." She smiled professionally. "Special occasion?"

Erika and Michael exchanged glances, a silent communication passing between them.

"Just a night away," Erika answered, her wedding ring catching the light as she accepted the keycards.

In the elevator, they stood closer than they had in months. Erika caught Michael's reflection in the mirrored wall—his jaw tense, eyes bright with anticipation. Neither spoke as they ascended, the soft hum of the elevator filling the space between them.

Room 718 was at the end of a long hallway. Michael's hand trembled slightly as he slid the keycard into the slot. The green light blinked, and he pushed the door open, stepping aside to let Erika enter first.

"It's beautiful," she murmured, taking in the expansive windows overlooking the city, the enormous bed draped in crisp white linens.

Michael set their bag down and checked his watch. "We have about an hour before..."

"Before he arrives," Erika finished for him. She moved to the minibar, extracting a small bottle of vodka. "Liquid courage?"

Michael nodded, accepting the drink she poured. Their fingers touched during the exchange, and neither pulled away immediately.

"Are you sure about this?" he asked, his voice low and serious. "We can still cancel."

Erika took a deliberate sip, feeling the alcohol warm her throat. "I'm nervous, but yes. I'm sure." She moved to the window, gazing out at the unfamiliar part of town. "It feels right somehow. Like we're finally being honest with each other."

Michael came up behind her, not quite touching. "I never thought we'd be here."

"Neither did I." She turned to face him. "But I'm glad we are."

Erika sipped her drink, remembering the night three weeks ago when they'd first created the profile together. They'd sat side by side on their bed, laptop balanced between them, the kids safely away at friends' houses.

"What should we write?" Michael had asked, cursor blinking in the empty "About Us" field.

"The truth," Erika had replied, surprising herself with her certainty. "That we're a married couple exploring together for the first time."

They'd debated every word of that profile, every boundary and preference. Michael preferred men with some experience. Erika wanted someone who wouldn't rush them. Both agreed their candidate needed to be discreet, respectful, and—above all—temporary.

"No locals," Michael had insisted. "Someone passing through."

"Someone who understands what this is," Erika had added. "And what it isn't."

They'd scrolled through dozens of profiles, dismissing most immediately. Too young. Too intense. Too many red flags in their messages. Each rejection had been a shared decision, each possibility discussed with unprecedented honesty between them.

Then David's profile appeared. Forty-two, business consultant, in town monthly for client meetings. His photo showed a confident smile, salt-and-pepper hair, athletic build. His description was straightforward: experienced with couples, understands discretion, prefers connection over casual encounters.

"Him," Erika had said immediately, something in his eyes resonating with her.

Michael had studied the profile longer, methodical as always. "Let's message him."

Their first video call with David had lasted two hours. He'd asked thoughtful questions about their expectations, their boundaries, their relationship. He'd shared his own experiences without bragging. When Michael hesitantly explained his bisexuality, David had nodded with understanding rather than judgment.

"You're both new to this," David had said. "We'll take it at whatever pace feels right."

The memory dissolved as Michael's phone chimed with a text notification. He glanced at the screen.

"It's him," Michael said. "He's in the lobby."

Erika felt her heartbeat quicken. "Tell him we'll be right down."

Michael typed the reply, then set his phone down. He reached for Erika's hand, squeezing it gently.

"Together?" he asked.

Erika nodded, squeezing back. "Together."

The hotel restaurant buzzed with quiet conversation and the gentle clink of silverware against porcelain. Erika smoothed her dress beneath her as she slid into the curved booth. Michael sat beside her, leaving space for their guest on his other side.

David appeared in the doorway, scanning the room. He looked exactly like his photos—tall with broad shoulders, silver threading through dark hair at his temples. When he spotted them, his smile revealed a slight dimple in his left cheek.

"Michael and Erika," he said, extending his hand first to Michael, then to Erika. "Even more attractive in person."

Michael cleared his throat. "We ordered wine. Red okay?"

"Perfect." David settled into his seat, unfolding his napkin with practiced ease.

The server appeared, pouring their wine and distributing menus. Silence descended as they studied the options, using the ritual as a buffer against the awkwardness hovering between them.

"So," Erika ventured after they'd ordered, "your work brings you here often?"

David nodded. "Corporate restructuring. Not exactly dinner conversation."

"Better than my accounting stories," Michael offered with a stiff laugh.

Erika took a long sip of wine, watching David over the rim of her glass. His fingers tapped lightly against the tablecloth—he was nervous too, despite his composed exterior.

"I have to ask," David said suddenly. "What made you two decide to try this? Most couples I've met, one person is dragging the other along. But you both seem equally invested."

Michael glanced at Erika, a silent question in his eyes. She nodded slightly.

"We realized we'd both been living secret lives," Michael explained, his voice low. "When everything came out, instead of destroying us, it opened up a conversation we should have had years ago."

"Honesty saved our marriage," Erika added. "Ironic, considering how many lies came before it."

David's expression softened. "That's actually beautiful."

Their appetizers arrived—a shared plate of seared scallops. David waited for them to take the first pieces.

"And your children?" he asked. "That's often the complicated part."

"They don't know," Erika said firmly. "They never will. This part of our lives is just for us."

"I respect that," David said, reaching for his wine glass. "My own rule is never to complicate people's lives."

Something in his sincerity broke the tension. Michael laughed genuinely at David's story about a disastrous business trip to Tokyo. Erika found herself leaning forward, drawn into their conversation about travel and architecture.

By the time their entrées arrived, the initial awkwardness had dissolved. David's hand occasionally brushed Michael's as they reached for the bread basket. Erika found herself admiring the way David listened intently when either of them spoke, his eyes crinkling at the corners when he smiled.

The elevator ride back to the room felt different—charged with anticipation rather than anxiety. Erika stood between the two men, hyper aware of David's cologne and Michael's familiar scent mingling in the enclosed space. No one spoke. The soft ding announcing their floor broke the silence.

Michael's hand trembled slightly as he unlocked the door. The room appeared different now—the king-sized bed no longer just furniture but the centerpiece of what was about to happen. David hung back, giving them space to enter first.

"Would anyone like a drink?" Michael asked, his voice slightly higher than normal.

"Water for me," David replied, removing his suit jacket and draping it carefully over a chair. "I prefer to stay clear-headed."

Erika kicked off her heels, suddenly conscious of the height difference between them all. She perched on the edge of the bed, watching Michael fill glasses at the minibar. His movements were precise, measured—his way of managing nervousness.

"This is strange," she admitted, breaking the tension. "Good strange, but still strange."

David smiled, remaining by the window. "It's okay to feel awkward. Most people do at first."

Michael handed out the drinks, then stood uncertainly in the middle of the room. Erika recognized the look on his face—the same expression he'd worn when they'd first discussed his attraction to men. Wanting but hesitant. Desire mixed with fear of judgment.

"I don't know how to start," Michael confessed, looking between them.

David nodded understandingly. "There's no script. We can talk more, or put on music, or..."

"Or we can just acknowledge this is new for all of us," Erika finished. She patted the bed beside her, inviting Michael to sit. When he did, she took his hand, threading her fingers through his. "I've never seen you with another man before."

Michael's breath caught. "I've never been with anyone while you watched."

They looked at each other with new eyes—not as the comfortable, familiar spouses they'd been for fifteen years, but as co-conspirators in this adventure. Partners in a different way.

David remained where he was, patient and observant. "This moment between you is beautiful," he said softly. "Take your time."

Erika squeezed Michael's hand, a silent signal passing between them. With their eyes locked together, they both turned to look at David, who offered a reassuring nod.

"Maybe we should start with something simple," Erika suggested, her voice a whisper of anticipation and nerves. "Just... talking for now."

David approached the bed, his movements smooth and unhurried. He sat down across from them, his gaze respectful yet filled with quiet interest. "Of course," he said. "Communication is key in these situations. Tell me what you're feeling, what you're comfortable with."

A beat of silence passed, filled only with the muffled sounds of the city below. Then Michael spoke up. "It's strange," he admitted. "I've wanted this for so long, but now that it's happening, I feel... exposed."

David offered a gentle smile. "That's completely normal," he assured them. "It's a big step, and it's okay to be nervous. The important thing is that we're all here, and we're all consenting adults. We can take this as slow as you need to."

Feeling emboldened by David's understanding, Erika reached out to touch his arm, the warmth of his skin radiating through the fabric of his shirt. "We appreciate your patience," she said. "This is new territory for us, but we're ready to explore."

With a nod of agreement, Michael leaned in to kiss Erika, the familiarity of his touch grounding her amidst the unknown. As their lips met, Erika felt a spark of desire ignite within her, fueled not just by the intimacy she shared with her husband, but by the knowledge that they were no longer confined to the boundaries of their marriage.

Breaking the kiss, Erika turned to David, her eyes conveying an unspoken invitation. The atmosphere in the room shifted, charged with a newfound excitement. Slowly, carefully, David closed the space between them, bringing his lips to Erika's in a tentative yet undeniably passionate kiss.

As Erika kissed David, she felt Michael's hand on her back, a tangible reminder of his presence and support. Encouraged by his touch, Erika reached out to explore the contours of David's chest with curious fingers, the solidity of his form both foreign and thrilling.

Michael watched, his gaze alternating between hunger and hesitation. Seeing his wife engage with another man stirred complex emotions within him, a mixture of arousal, jealousy, and a profound sense of liberation.

Erika broke away from David, turning back to Michael. "Your turn," she said softly, her eyes shining with a combination of daring and affection.

With a deep breath, Michael leaned in, closing the distance to David. Their lips met in a kiss that was cautious at first, but quickly deepened as the initial awkwardness gave way to an undeniable attraction.

Erika watched, her heart pounding with a cocktail of emotions—excitement, love, and an intense arousal at the sight of her husband embracing another man. It was a side of Michael she had never seen, and the vulnerability and passion he displayed were both a revelation and a powerful aphrodisiac.

The rest of the night unfolded in a series of gentle explorations, each touch and kiss building upon the last. There was no rush, no sense of urgency—just a shared desire to discover the boundaries of their newfound sexual freedom.

Together, they navigated the uncharted waters of their desires, their actions guided by mutual respect and a genuine connection. It was a night of firsts, of breaking down walls and building new bridges, of redefining what it meant to be adventurous, open, and honest in their marriage.

As the early morning light began to filter through the curtains, the three of them lay entwined on the bed, each lost in their own thoughts. They had crossed a threshold that night, stepping into a world that they had only dared to imagine before. And as they held each other in the quiet aftermath, it was clear that their journey had only just begun.

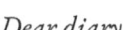

Dear diary,

Last night with David changed everything. Not just the sex—though that was incredible—but seeing Michael in this new light. His nervousness surprised me. The man who's always so composed at work, who handles our finances with military precision, was trembling slightly when David first touched him.

There was something so vulnerable, so genuine about it. His eyes kept finding mine, seeking reassurance. I'd forgotten how beautiful his eyes are when they're filled with uncertainty and desire. It reminded me of our early days, when everything between us was new and overwhelming.

I realized I've missed that version of my husband—the one who isn't entirely sure of himself, who needs me as much as I need him. Watching him navigate these uncharted waters, seeing his careful hesitation bloom into hunger... it awakened something I thought was dead between us.

Pure joy. That's what I felt. Not just pleasure or excitement, but actual joy—with my husband. That feeling I'd lost so long ago came rushing back, and I could see in his eyes that Michael felt it too. We were discovering each other all over again, through this shared experience.

After David left our hotel room, something shifted even further. Michael locked the door and turned to me with an intensity I haven't seen in years. He didn't speak—didn't need to. He crossed the room in three strides and was on me before I could catch my breath.

He was an animal. He took me against the wall, then on the floor, finally on the bed again. There was no hesitation, no polite question about whether I was in the mood. He was filled with a newfound desire for me that had been absent for so long.

It wasn't just about the physical release. It was about reclaiming each other after sharing ourselves with someone else. Proving that what we have together is still powerful, still essential, a bond so strong, even as we open ourselves to new experiences.

For the first time in years, I fell asleep feeling truly wanted by my husband. Not tolerated, not obligated to, but desperately wanted.

The following week, Zach bounded down the stairs and skidded into the kitchen where I was finishing breakfast preparations.

He froze, blinking at the spread of eggs, bacon, and fresh-cut fruit.

"Whoa. Did someone die or something?" He grabbed a piece of bacon. "You haven't made breakfast on a Tuesday since... I don't even remember."

I laughed, swatting his hand playfully. "Can't a mother cook for her family without a national emergency?"

Lily appeared in the doorway, her skeptical gaze sweeping from the food to me, then to Michael who was humming—actually humming—while pouring coffee.

"Dad's home for breakfast too?" She slid onto a stool. "Okay, what's happening? Are we moving? Are you guys getting divorced?"

Michael and I exchanged quick glances, a silent conversation passing between us. The kind we used to have before everything went sideways.

"We're not getting divorced," Michael said, setting a mug in front of me, his fingers lingering against mine. "Quite the opposite."

Zach rolled his eyes. "Gross, Dad."

"We've just..." I searched for the right words. "We've realized we weren't spending enough time together. As a family."

Michael nodded. "Work isn't going anywhere. But you two—" he gestured with his coffee mug, "—are growing up too fast."

Later that evening, I found Lily sitting on the porch swing, scrolling through her phone. I joined her, and we swayed in comfortable silence for a moment.

"Mom?" She didn't look up. "Are you guys really okay now? Because before, it felt like..."

"Like what, honey?"

She shrugged. "Like you were ghosts or something. Like you were here, but not really here."

I pulled her close, surprised when she didn't resist. "I'm sorry if it felt that way. Your dad and I... we had some things to figure out."

"And you figured them out?"

I thought about the new understanding between Michael and me, the shared secrets, the unexpected joy we'd rediscovered.

"We're working on it," I said honestly. "But yes, I think we're finding our way back."

That night, Michael and I sat at the kitchen table long after the kids went to bed, planning a weekend camping trip—something we hadn't done in years. His hand found mine across the table, warm and certain.

CHAPTER FORTY

New Chapter

Six months later

    I traced my finger over the leather-bound diary, feeling the slight indentations from hundreds of entries. The pages had witnessed my darkest moments, my spiral into compulsion, and now, my recovery.

Dear diary,

Six months since Michael and I laid our secrets bare. Sometimes I still catch myself staring at my phone, that familiar itch crawling beneath my skin when Michael works late or when I'm alone too long. But the difference now is that I recognize it for what it is - not desire, but escape. The compulsion has faded from a roaring demand to a distant whisper.

Last weekend's encounter with James was different from anything before. Michael knew. We discussed boundaries before-

hand. I wasn't hiding or running. I was simply experiencing. No shame shadowed the pleasure, no frantic need to fill some bottomless void. Just connection, freely chosen.

I closed the diary as laughter erupted from the dining room. Michael was telling that ridiculous story about the camping trip disaster - the one where Zach accidentally used poison oak as toilet paper. I slipped the diary into my desk drawer and joined my family.

"Mom, please make him stop," Lily groaned, her face flushed with embarrassment and suppressed laughter.

"I don't know," I said, sliding back into my chair. "It's a pretty good story."

Michael's hand found mine across the table, our fingers intertwining naturally. The gesture didn't escape Zach's notice.

"You guys are so weird lately," he said, stabbing a potato. "Always touching and laughing at stuff that isn't even funny."

Lily nodded. "It's like you have all these inside jokes now."

Michael squeezed my hand. "Is it so strange that your mother and I enjoy each other's company?"

Later, after the kids retreated to their rooms with mumbled goodnights and the clatter of devices, Michael and I settled on the patio with generous glasses of merlot. The night air wrapped around us like a comfortable blanket, carrying the scent of jasmine from the corner of the garden.

"James texted," I said, watching the moonlight catch in my wine. "He's in town next month. Wants to meet up."

Michael nodded, swirling his wine thoughtfully, the ruby liquid catching the glow from the string lights overhead. "How do you feel about that?"

"Interested, but not desperate." I took a deliberate sip, savoring the rich flavor. "It's different now. And you? How's David?"

"We're meeting for coffee next week." His eyes met mine, clear and honest, no shadows between us. "Just coffee. Nothing more."

"Our boundaries still working for you?" I asked, studying his face for any hint of reservation.

He reached for my hand, his thumb tracing small circles on my skin. "They are. You?"

"Yes," I said simply, feeling the truth of it settle in my chest. "I never thought I'd say this, but I'm... content. Not perfect, not solved, just... genuinely content and happy."

Later that night, I added one final line to my diary entry:

We found freedom... not in perfect fidelity, but in perfect honesty.

About Julie Freebush

Passionate and Dedicated

Ever wondered what it's like to live a life filled with passion, desire, and forbidden love?

Meet Julie Freebush, the author who knows no bounds when it comes to exploring the realms of *eroticism*.

Julie has had an intense fascination with *seduction* and *temptation* since her childhood, when an innocent skinny dipping experience sparked something deep inside her.

Her stories are filled with *seduction*, *temptation*, and *illicit encounters* that will leave you *breathless*.

Julie spends her days *writing* and her nights "*Researching*".

As an author who knows no bounds.

Julie's experiences range from the *scandalous* to the down-right *explicit*, and her writing is a testament to her *insatiable appetite for pleasure*.

Julie's works are filled with *secrets, lust, and explicit encounters* that will leave your heart racing. So, if you're ready to embark on a journey of *sensuality* and *illicit pleasure*, join *Julie Freebush* in her world of *Short & Steamy Tales of Erotica.*

For all the latest releases and current happenings with Julie, stop by her website.   JulieFreeb ush.com

Also by Julie Freebush

Savage Tides: Survival and Desire

Julie's Unabridged ADULT Research Stories Series

Short and Steamy Tales of Erotica:

Volumes One & Two

Home From the Army: Book One An Erotic Tale of Passion, Seduction, Family and Forbidden Desires